Xander
and the Pen

To my two (much wiser) sisters

First published 2023

EK Books
an imprint of Exisle Publishing Pty Ltd
PO Box 864, Chatswood, NSW 2057, Australia
226 High Street, Dunedin, 9016, New Zealand

A CiP record for this book is available from the National Library of Australia.

ISBN 978-1-922539-40-3

Designed by Mark Thacker
Typeset in Minion Pro 12 on 18 pt
Printed in China

This book uses paper sourced under ISO 14001 guidelines from well-managed forests and other controlled sources.

10 9 8 7 6 5 4 3 2 1

Xander and the Pen

DAVID LAWRENCE

ILLUSTRATED BY CHERIE DIGNAM

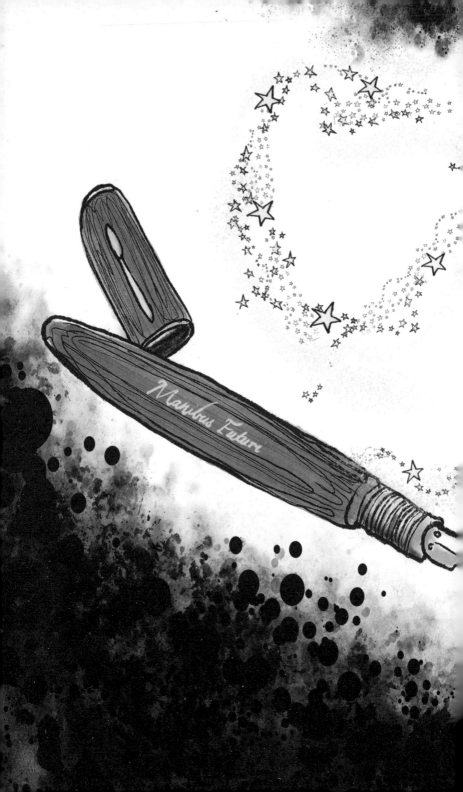

CHAPTER

The sound of the creaky classroom door being opened made Xander spin around. It took nearly a second for his gigantic mop of curly brown hair to catch up with his tiny head.

Standing in the doorway was Timmy Fontaine, the second-smallest kid in Xander's year. Tears streamed down his face and rivulets of bright red blood trickled from his nose. Several buttons were missing from his tattered white shirt, which was covered in twigs and random patches of dirt.

Xander looked back to the front of the class, where Mr Steele was standing next to the whiteboard. The bald-headed teacher with a heavily waxed moustache narrowed his eyes and folded his arms.

'What happened to you, Fontaine?' he said.

'Um, I kind of tripped, sir,' said Timmy.

'Well, I can't have you bleeding all over one of *my* desks!'

Xander rolled his eyes and Mr Steele glared at him.

'Got something to say, Beeston?' he snapped.

'No sir,' replied Xander. He meekly bowed his head and stared at his desk.

'I didn't think so,' sneered the teacher. 'Fontaine, go to sick bay *immediately*, and get yourself cleaned up.'

As soon as Timmy was gone, Mr Steele turned to scribble more unsolvable maths problems onto the whiteboard. Well, unsolvable to Xander. He looked across at his mate Tee-Jay, who was writing down the answers as quickly as the questions appeared.

Xander widened his eyes in mock surprise, causing the raven-haired girl seated next to him to smile.

'Don't make me laugh!' whispered Cat.

Xander put his hand on his heart and mouthed, 'Who me?'

Cat snorted out loud, and Mr Steele whirled around like an angry scorpion.

'Something amusing you, Miss Cruz?'

'No sir … something got caught in my throat.'

'Well if anything else gets caught in your throat, *everyone* will be staying back after school! Got it?'

'Yes sir,' said Cat.

After Mr Steele turned back to the whiteboard, Xander looked at Cat and mouthed, 'I am *so* disappointed in you!'

His friend barely managed to hold back a secondary snort. Xander grinned and pulled out a blank piece of paper. He then reached into his mass of hair to retrieve a pencil from behind his ear and set to work.

Just before the end of the school day the classroom door opened again, letting in a welcome blast of cool, fresh sea air. In limped Timmy Fontaine holding an icepack. His eyes were puffy and he was wearing a Dukescliff Primary and Middle School windcheater that was at least four sizes too big.

Xander guessed the top had been 'borrowed' from the lost and found bin located next to the sick bay.

As Timmy hobbled towards his desk, Mr Steele acknowledged his return with a disinterested grunt. Less than a minute later, the sound of the bell sent students scurrying for the exit, like rats escaping from a sinking ship.

'Don't forget your homework!' yelled Mr Steele without even looking up from his table.

Xander noticed that Timmy had remained seated, so he walked over.

'Was it the Bruise Brothers?' he asked Timmy.

Timmy nodded nervously.

Xander nodded back and handed over the sketch he had

The bruise brothers are ......toast!

completed instead of solving Mr Steele's equations. A smile instantly appeared on Timmy's face.

'That is *awesome!*'

The cartoon drawing was of a musclebound Timmy wearing a fluttering superhero cape. He was standing triumphantly on top of Tony and Jeff Clagg, or as they liked to call themselves, 'The Bruise Brothers'. But instead of giving the Clagg boys normal bodies, Xander had made the bullies into pieces of toast, with little arms, legs and heads sticking out. Down the bottom was the caption: 'The Bruise Brothers are … toast!'

'Thanks, "Beast"!' said Timmy. 'You're a legend.'

Xander's face turned the colour of a hydroponic tomato.

'Better go — Tee-Jay and Cat are waiting for me,' Xander said before grabbing his bag and rushing out the door.

Xander quickly spotted his friends chatting underneath a giant Monterey cypress tree. In the background was Cygnet Bay and, as he jogged over, a wedge of black swans launched majestically off the water.

'You nearly got me into so much trouble!' said Cat.

'What? I did not say one *word* to make you laugh.'

'You don't have to … you have a very funny face.'

'Funny in a *cool* way, right?'

'Let's just leave it at "funny",' said Cat.

Tee-Jay burst out laughing and Xander turned to him and sighed.

'I expected more from you, mate,' he said. 'And because you just laughed at me, I'm *not* going to help you with your maths homework!'

'Not that, Beast! Anything but that!' pleaded Tee-Jay.

The three friends started walking towards the gate, when a voice called out from the school's outdoor basketball court.

'You want to shoot some hoops?'

A girl with short spikey hair bounced the basketball a few times before throwing the ball over her head to make a spectacular shot.

'All net, Phoebe!' screamed Cat, throwing down her bag and racing over to the court. 'I'm in!'

'Me too!' said Tee-Jay.

'How about you Xander?' asked Phoebe.

'Sorry, sis, got a weightlifting session at four — need to keep these guns loaded!'

Xander started posing like a bodybuilder then added, 'They don't call me "The Beast" for nothing.'

'I'm pretty sure they do!' countered Tee-Jay.

'Yeah — you're the least beastly person I know,' said Cat.

Ignoring his friends' comments, Xander put on a dramatic voice, just like the ones used in American movie trailers.

'Xander Beeston — by day, a mild mannered, 40-kilogram weakling, but whenever there's a full moon, he becomes … The Beast!'

Cat had to sit down she was laughing so hard.

'I'd like to see that!' yelled Tee-Jay.

'Oh, you'll see it my friend — just wait till the next full moon! Ar-woooooo!'

'OMG, Xander! You sound like a chihuahua!' laughed Phoebe, spinning her wheelchair around to face him.

He watched his little sister sink a long range three-point shot and smiled proudly.

'See you two tomorrow, and see you at home, Phoebs.'

Xander pulled his bag over his shoulders like a backpack, and started whistling as he headed out the rusty old gate.

Straight away, Xander knew he was in danger. He didn't need a superhero's special sixth sense to alert him — Tony Clagg's menacing voice was a dead giveaway.

'There he is. Let's get him!'

CHAPTER

2

Xander froze.

Beads of sweat appeared on his forehead, and he felt like a hyperactive rubber ball was trying to escape from inside his chest.

'You're *so* dead!' yelled Jeff Clagg.

If Xander had superpowers he would have faced his foes and declared, 'There's no such thing as "*so*" dead, Jeff. You're either alive, or you're dead … as you're about to find out!' But Xander didn't have superpowers, so he ran away instead. He set off along Hinchinbrook Road, before turning down Grange Avenue where the houses were known for their colourful, flower-filled gardens and neatly trimmed box hedges.

But there was no time to appreciate the eye-catching orange and red hibiscus or the bright pink and purple fuchsias, because the Bruise Brothers were only ten seconds behind him, and closing. Xander wished he had his sister's speed. Well … her speed before the accident. He also wished he had her courage.

A thought suddenly popped into his head, and he turned left into the zigzagging St Hubert's Street. Just after the street jagged left, Xander ducked down a tiny side road named Yal Yal Lane, and kept sprinting. Seconds later he heard the frustrated shouts of the Bruise Brothers.

'Where is he?'

'The little skunk must have slipped down Yal Yal!'

Xander's clever tactic gained him twenty seconds, but he doubted it would be enough.

Once out of Yal Yal Lane, he ran directly towards the ocean. He could see the large expanse of blue water in the distance, but it appeared smaller than usual. And it seemed to be shrinking. He blinked a few times before realizing that an eerie, low-level mist was rolling towards shore. It looked like it was swallowing the sea.

Behind him the pounding sound of the Bruise Brothers' feet grew louder, and that's when he saw the giant banner.

DUKESCLIFF MARKET OPEN TODAY!

In the distance he could see people milling around the makeshift stalls set up in Wakefield Park. As he propelled himself forward, the welcoming aroma of barbecued onions and sausages teased his nose.

Xander's pursuers were closing on him as he sped through the market's entrance and began weaving between the laidback locals.

'Give up, Beast!' yelled Jeff.

'Yeah, you're only making things worse!' roared Tony.

Suddenly the temperature plunged and Xander couldn't see anything. It was as if someone had turned off the sun. The thick mist had made it to shore, instantly enveloping the entire marketplace.

Xander dropped to his knees. Just before losing visibility, he had spotted a line of portable toilets to his left, and he began crawling in that direction so he could hide around the back of them.

But the sound of the Bruise Brothers' voices made him stop in his tracks.

'Where'd he go?' asked Jeff.

'Dunno — he was right here,' replied Tony.

'Let's hold hands so we don't get split up,' suggested Jeff.

'I'm not holding your hand!'

'I was joking!'

'Yeah right! Let's check from here up to the end of the row. Even though we can't see him, he can't be far away.'

Xander held his breath as Tony's angry face loomed through the fog — his head appeared to be floating without a body. It then vanished into the mist just as quickly as it had appeared.

Xander let out a deep sigh and resumed crawling. Unfortunately, he slightly misjudged the distance and ended up locating the toilets with his head. 'Ouch!' he said. Ignoring the pain, he felt his way around the back and lay down on his stomach. As he caught his breath, he could hear younger kids screaming and adults cursing as they bumped into each other.

Over the loudspeakers a woman with a calming voice announced, 'No need to panic, everyone. For safety reasons please stay exactly where you are — the mist should clear in about fifteen minutes.'

Xander knew he had to escape before the cover of the fog disappeared. As he stood up, his left hand pressed against something on the ground. It was money — notes and coins. The mist was too thick for Xander to see how much cash was there, but he gratefully stuffed it into his pocket.

He set off waving his hands in front of him so he could detect any obstacles before colliding with them. Lots of people had turned on the torches on their phones, so he carefully avoided any luminous circles of light that permeated the grey mass surrounding him.

The fog's density began to lighten, and this helped him gain his bearings. The exit was now fairly close, but just as he was about to slip away a golden flash of light caught his attention. Xander glanced towards the source of the light but then fought off his curiosity and crept towards the Wakefield Park gates. He could now make out the outlines of the market stalls, so he knew he had to keep moving.

Another even bigger golden flash suddenly erupted, and it seemed to come from the stall at the end of the row. Xander was intrigued. Despite the risk, he decided to sneak over and find out what was going on.

After squinting at the sign above the stall, he mouthed, 'Second-hand Treasures'.

He could vaguely make out an unusual assortment of objects on the unsteady trestle table: antique lamps, a variety of colourful crystals and … a pen.

Even in the poor light he could tell it was a very old pen. It was scratched and battered but had striking gold writing on the side. Xander didn't know why, but he felt drawn to it. His hand trembled as he reached out to pick it up and …

Zap!

A warm surge of power flowed from the pen into Xander's fingers, then up his arm before spreading throughout his entire body. In an instant he felt safe, like he was wearing a protective layer of armour.

'Nothing can harm me,' he whispered. He smiled as he stared at the pen and tried to make sense of the strange writing on its side.

'*Manibus futuri.*'

'That's Latin,' said a deep voice from the other side of the table. Xander's head jerked up to see an old man wearing a purple robe covered in yellow moons and stars, with a matching circular hat. The skin on his face looked like well-worn leather, and his eyes sparkled with mischief.

'S-s-sorry?' replied Xander.

'The writing on the pen — it's Latin,' said the man.

'Latin?'

'An ancient language.'

Xander re-examined the words.

'Man-i-bus fu-tur-i,' he said.

'It means, "The future is in your hands",' explained the elderly man. 'If you're interested in buying it, it's …'

He put his hand on his chin and looked Xander up and down, before giving a small nod. '… Fifteen dollars and forty cents.'

Xander gently replaced the pen on the table. 'Um, no thanks,' he said. 'I don't have any money.'

'That's a pity,' said the man.

Xander dejectedly shoved his hand into his pocket, and was instantly reminded of his discovery behind the portable toilets.

'Hang on! I *do* have money!' he said, as he started pulling the cash from his pocket and counting it on the trestle table.

'There's ten dollars, and, um, hang on, there's another five … and twenty cents, and another ten … and here's five more — how much is that?'

'That's fifteen dollars and thirty-five cents,' said the man. 'You're five cents short.'

Xander's face dropped.

'Are you sure there's no more money in your pocket?' asked the man.

Xander delved back into his pocket and fished around again.

'No … wait a sec!' With a beaming smile, Xander pulled out another five-cent piece.

'Fifteen dollars forty exactly!' he said.

'Excellent. Now it's an ink pen, so you'll need some ink …'

At this, Xander folded his arms and glared at the purple-robed salesman.

'Don't worry,' the man reassured Xander, 'the ink is included in the price.'

Xander let out a small sigh, as the man handed him an ornate bottle filled with a dark liquid.

'Thanks!' he said. He quickly unzipped his school bag and put the pen and bottle of ink inside.

'No, thank *you*,' said the mysterious man.

Xander was so excited, he failed to notice the mist had almost completely disappeared. On reaching the exit, he turned to have another look at the 'Second-hand Treasures' stall.

But it wasn't where he thought it should be, and he started scanning the marketplace to find it.

Suddenly Xander felt his arms being grabbed.

'Gotcha!' announced Tony Clagg.

'Yeah — it's payback time!' said his younger brother.

'But I didn't do anything!' pleaded Xander.

'Really?' said Tony. 'What about this?'

The bully held up the drawing Xander had given Timmy Fontaine. It was now covered in spots of blood … presumably Timmy's.

'So we're toast, are we?' said Jeff. 'Well, if *we're* toast, then you're, um, you're …'

'Yeah, that would make you the, errr …' said Tony.

As the Claggs struggled to come up with a killer metaphor, Xander shut his eyes and mentally drew a cartoon of himself as a musclebound superhero with a giant 'T' on his chest. He was shooting flames at the Bruise Brothers, depicted as pieces of toast, with the caption: 'You're the toast and I'm … "The Toaster"!'

Five minutes later, as they approached a grey brick toilet block by the beach, the Bruise Brothers were still struggling with their 'toast-related' word play.

'… So hang on, is *Xander* the toast, or are *we* the toast?' asked Jeff.

'I think we're the toast, so he's like the … butter, maybe?'

'Because butter squishes? So … would it be better if he was *margarine*? That squishes even easier …'

'Don't worry about it, we're here,' said Tony gruffly. 'Now go and check if the coast is clear.'

'The coast? As in the beach?'

Tony rolled his eyes.

'No, the loos!'

'Oh!' Jeff ducked inside the old toilet block, then quickly reappeared. 'No one's here!' he declared.

'Excellent,' said Tony, pushing Xander roughly in front of him.

Xander was bustled into the larger disabled cubicle and Jeff shut the door, locking it behind them.

'Today we're going to give you a Bruise Brothers specialty,' announced Tony. 'The Royal Flush!'

Xander was terrified, but his curiosity got the better of him.

'So … you guys have names for all the mean things you do?'

'Oh yeah,' said Jeff proudly. 'We've got the Sock and Roll, the Hedge of Darkness, the Sand Wedgie …'

'Stop giving away trade secrets!' hissed Tony.

He turned to Xander and held up the bloodied drawing.

'This is why you must pay.'

The bullies grabbed Xander by the shoulders, ripping his shirt as they dragged his head towards the toilet bowl.

'Damn! It's a clean one,' moaned Jeff.

Xander sighed, but his relief was short-lived as his head was pushed downwards, then hit with a liquid explosion as Tony pressed the flush button.

The Bruise Brothers howled with laughter as Xander spluttered out water that felt as if it had reached the base of his lungs.

'What's that, Beast? You want another ride? Okay then!' said Tony.

Xander felt the pressure reapplied to the back of his head, and once again he was subjected to the Royal Flush. He was then dragged back so that he was sitting with his knees to his

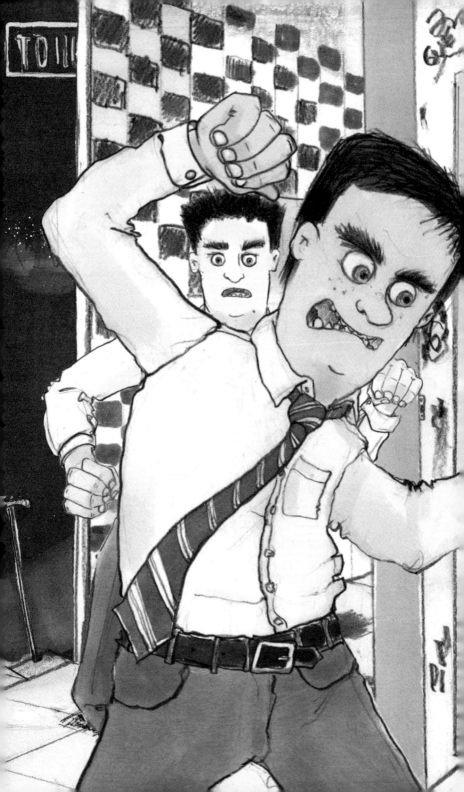

chest and his back to the cubicle door.

'Beast, with your hair you'd make a good toilet brush,' suggested Tony.

'Nah, his hair's too soft — you need those hard-plastic bristly bits …'

'It was a joke, Jeff!'

'Oh yeah — good one.'

Xander let out a small sigh. *At least it's over*, he thought.

'Let's check out what's in his bag,' suggested Tony.

Xander's eyebrows shot skywards, telling the bullies all they needed to know.

'Oooh, there's definitely something in there he's worried about,' squealed Jeff.

Tony tipped up the bag and the pen and bottle of ink fell onto the floor.

Instinctively Xander reached out to grab them, but Jeff was too quick.

'I think we need another flush!'

'Agreed,' said Tony with a cruel smile.

Xander looked on as Jeff opened the ink jar and tipped its blue contents into the toilet. After placing the empty bottle and the pen into the bowl, he raised his right hand and extended his pointer finger.

'Noooooooo!' yelled Xander.

'Serves you right, Beast,' said Tony. 'You do a nasty drawing of us, and we destroy one of your stupid pens.'

Jeff pushed the button and the roaring, flushing sound started up straight away.

'Our work here is done,' announced Tony.

The Bruise Brothers gave each other a high five, before unlocking the cubicle door and leaving in fits of laughter.

Xander immediately raced over and stared hopefully into the toilet.

But apart from a small pool of water, it was completely empty.

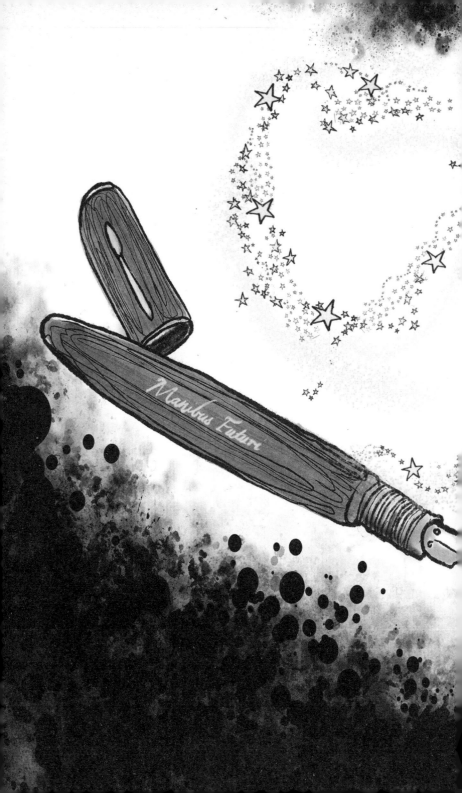

CHAPTER

3

Xander walked home with tears in his eyes.

His shoulders throbbed with pain and the Royal Flush had been humiliating, but all he could think about was the beautiful pen that was gone forever.

As he approached the Black Lighthouse situated on Vicar's Bluff, his spirits lifted. It was a striking, unmanned lighthouse made of perfectly cut blocks of bluestone.

'Bluestone? How come it's not called the *Blue* Lighthouse?' he had once asked his father. His dad responded as he always did when he didn't know the answer: 'Google it!'

Xander stopped and stared at the elegant structure as thin wisps of mist hovered around its base. He pursed his lips, then took a sketch pad from his bag. After sitting down he started creating a new character called 'Lighthouse Girl'. In his sketch, a powerful-looking girl wearing a superhero suit with LG on the chest, was assisting a ship being attacked by a giant octopus. Her headband had a round light on it, which lit up the scene. As the flying Lighthouse Girl grabbed one of the creature's huge tentacles, she said, 'Stop Squid-ding Around!'

Xander smiled, replaced the pencil behind his ear, and packed his cartoon away. He set off for home and started to whistle. But the whistling stopped when he spotted the 'Clagg's Cannery' sign that stood in front of an ugly, grey, box-shaped factory.

Xander broke into a quick jog and soon approached the footbridge that linked Dukescliff to the other side of Cygnet Bay. A high-pitched whine carried through the air, causing him to stop and cock his ear. But all he could hear was the familiar warble of a magpie in a nearby pine tree.

He shrugged his shoulders and was about to move off when the whining started up again. He peered under the bridge and let out a gasp as a set of eyes materialized out of the darkness.

He froze as the creature moved towards him and into the light. It was a dog. The mangiest dog Xander had ever seen. Its hair appeared to be reddish brown with patches of white - although it was so matted, it was hard to tell. The pooch was skin and bones, and Xander could smell it had not had a bath for some time. But the dog's most concerning

Stop Squid-ding Around!

characteristic was that it was shivering uncontrollably.

The mutt looked up at Xander with brown, soulful eyes, and started whimpering.

'What's wrong, girl?'

The dog barked and rolled over onto its back.

'Oops, I mean *boy*,' said Xander.

He moved closer and slowly extended his hand, causing the dog to jump back to his feet. Xander narrowed his eyes and scanned the mutt from head to toe.

'You got something in your mouth?'

He kept his hand extended and inched closer, causing the trembling hound to let out a small growl.

'If you bite me, can you please give me "super dog" powers?' Xander tried to imagine what that would be like. In his mind he drew a picture of a superhero called 'Woof Boy', trapping a couple of rough-looking criminals in a giant pool of drool.

He was imagining Woof Boy saying, 'Your crime spree has come to a sticky end!' when the dog's whimpering snapped him out of his daydream. Xander was now close enough to reach out and touch the scraggy canine.

'Steady boy, steady', he said, leaning forward and gently stroking the distressed dog's head.

'There you go, shh.'

He slowly moved his hands down to the dog's mouth and gently started to prise it open.

'That's it.'

Straight away Xander could see a sturdy twig lodged in the trembling dog's mouth. As carefully as possible, he started manoeuvring the trapped stick backwards and forwards, and up and down.

'Here it comes, here it comes and ...'

The twig gave way and Xander slowly pulled it from his patient's mouth. It was coated in a bloody glob of saliva, and he quickly tossed it behind him.

He wasn't sure which of them was more surprised at the operation's success, but the dog's wagging tail signalled he'd made a friend for life.

'So ... what should I call you?' The dog lay down and began shivering like he was inside a refrigerator. This gave Xander an idea.

'How about ... Shiver?' The dog raised his head and gave a friendly bark.

'Shiver it is!'

Xander reached into his bag and retrieved his lunchbox. Inside was half a ham-and-cheese sandwich that he offered to Shiver. The famished dog didn't bother sniffing it, scoffing the snack down in two rapid-fire bites.

Xander then took out his sports T-shirt. As usual, he had barely raised a sweat in PE class that day, so it was bone dry. He rubbed the shirt over Shiver's fur and could feel the dog warming up. And as he put away his lunchbox and filthy T-shirt in his bag, Shiver nuzzled under his arm.

A few minutes later Xander stood to leave, and his new four-legged friend started barking.

'Don't worry, mate,' he reassured the dog, 'I'll be back later.' He gave Shiver a quick scratch behind the ear, then checked his watch.

'Oops — I really have to go!'

He jogged off at a steady pace and fifteen minutes later arrived at his family's modest house in Quarry Street. Xander loved living in Quarry Street. The neighbours all got on extremely well and every December his parents organized a popular street party.

Xander opened the wooden gate and walked along the uneven brick footpath that split the well-maintained lawn. He headed up the short ramp, quietly opened the front door and tiptoed inside.

'Xander, is that you?'

'Um, yes Mum — just going to my room …'

Almost instantly, Mrs Beeston appeared in the hallway with her hands on her hips. Xander had no idea how his mother did it, but if he or his sister were ever up to mischief, she would materialize out of thin air like a ninja. He had even created a cartoon character called 'Ninja Mum', a mind-reading superhero with phenomenal hearing, who could always tell when people were lying.

'What happened to you?'

'Nothing …'

Mrs Beeston stared at Xander and crossed her arms. 'Your hair's a mess, your eyes are puffy, your shirt's ripped, and "nothing" happened?'

Before Xander could respond, Phoebe wheeled into the hallway, followed by their balding father.

'What's going on?' asked Mr Beeston.

'I don't want to say,' replied Xander. 'You'll make a big deal out of it and make things worse.'

'Spill!' said Mrs Beeston.

Xander took a deep breath.

'Jeff and Tony … they … didn't like a drawing I did and they kind of … flushed my head down a toilet.'

Phoebe's face went bright red.

'They did *what*?' Mrs Beeston turned to her husband. 'Cam?'

'Right, I'm going around to the Claggs' place to sort this out.'

'Dad, noooooo!' begged Xander.

'All I'm going to do is have a "father to father" chat with Tristan — that's how adults deal with these situations.'

Mr Beeston grabbed his car keys off the old dresser in the hallway and headed out the front door. He turned back and stared at Xander.

'Well, come on!'

'What do you mean?' said Xander, panicking.

'You're coming with me.'

'No way!'

'You can stay in the car, but you're coming with me. Now!'

Xander rolled his eyes and trudged outside. He followed his dad to the rusty old lime-green station wagon parked on the street and hopped into the front passenger seat.

'Dad, let's just *pretend* to go. Mr Clagg's your boss, and you know what he's like.'

'That doesn't matter. His boys are out of control and he needs to sort them out.' With that, Mr Beeston put the car into drive and headed around to The Boulevard.

The Boulevard was the most exclusive street in Dukescliff. It contained only eight houses — all double storey with sweeping views of the ocean out the front, and wonderful outlooks over Cygnet Bay at the rear. The Claggs lived at number 4, a freshly painted white wooden house with an imposing veranda on the second floor. The property was fronted by a giant manicured green hedge instead of a fence.

Mr Beeston drove the station wagon into the driveway and parked it behind a gleaming blue sports car.

'Stay here,' he said to Xander. He unclipped his seatbelt, hopped out and walked along the white pebble path to the enormous double doors at the front of the house.

Xander slumped down in the seat, but wound down the window so he could hear better. He watched his dad push the bell then wait for at least a minute before the door opened. The hulking frame of Mr Clagg emerged, and he did not look happy.

'What do you want?' he demanded.

'I want to talk to you about your boys, Tristan. They flushed my son's head down a toilet.'

Xander went bright red and wriggled further down in the seat.

'Boys!' yelled Mr Clagg. 'Get down here … now!' He folded his arms and glared at Mr Beeston in silence.

Jeff and Tony appeared in the doorway — they were almost as tall as Xander's father.

'Did either of you flush Xander's head down a toilet?'

'No, Dad,' said Tony.

'He, um fell in,' said Jeff. Tony elbowed his younger brother in the ribs and gave him a withering look.

'You can't possibly believe that, Tristan,' said Mr Beeston.

Xander watched Mr Clagg puff out his chest and move forward so that he was towering over his father.

'Are you calling my boys liars?'

Mr Beeston paused for a moment, weighing up what to say.

'No … I'm calling them liars *and* bullies.'

Mr Clagg gave Mr Beeston an enormous shove, leaving him sprawled on the perfectly clipped lawn.

'How dare you come here and insult my family?' he roared. 'You know what? You're fired … and so is Betty!'

Xander felt sick. Both his parents had just been sacked … because of him.

'Now get off my property!' yelled Mr Clagg.

He then pushed his boys inside and slammed the door shut.

Mr Beeston picked himself up, wiped off the grass and returned to the station wagon.

'That went well,' he said.

At dinner, Xander didn't feel like talking or eating. He stared at the roast lamb and pushed his peas around the plate.

'You should eat that,' suggested Mrs Beeston with a smile. 'We might not be able to afford another roast for a while.'

'It's so unfair,' said Phoebe.

'We'll be right, Phoebs. I'll catch us fish every day,' said Mr Beeston. 'And don't forget, there's every chance I'll discover Finito's treasure with "The Seeker"!'

Xander's eyes shot across to his father's metal detector, nicknamed The Seeker, sitting in the corner. A smile returned to his face.

'So, Dad, how did you come up with the name The Seeker?' he asked innocently.

'It just popped into my head one day.'

'So it has *nothing* to do with Harry Potter's Quidditch position?' asked Phoebe.

'Who's Harry Potter?'

'It's interesting that you came up with that nickname a few days after my *Harry Potter and the Goblet of Fire* went missing,' pointed out Xander.

'I have no idea what you're talking about,' said Mr Beeston.

'Dad you are the *worst* liar,' laughed Phoebe. 'You would be in Slytherin for sure.'

'No way! The Sorting Hat would have sent me straight into Gryffindor … I mean, what's a Slytherin?'

'You are so busted, Dad!'

'Anyway, the point is The Seeker and I are going to find Finito's buried treasure ... have I ever told you about Finito's treasure?'

'Yes!' said Xander.

'Okay, I'll tell you all about it then. There was this pirate called Finito who was one of the most cunning pirates to ever—'

'Sail the seven seas,' said Xander and Phoebe in unison.

'It's almost like I've told this story before ...'

'You have!' said Xander.

'Like a million times!' added Phoebe.

Mrs Beeston snorted, then started laughing into her napkin.

Mr Beeston ignored the interjections and continued his history lesson.

'Legend has it that Finito and his crew stole a treasure chest filled with priceless jewels and buried it somewhere around Dukescliff. But before he could come back to dig it up, his ship crashed into rocks, and he and his entire crew perished without a trace. And so, until this day, Finito's treasure is—'

'Still waiting to be found!' said all four of them together.

After everyone had stopped laughing, Xander looked around at his family and smiled.

Later on as he helped clear the table, he smuggled some slices of lamb from his plate and crammed them into his pocket.

'Good to see you got your appetite back,' said Mrs Beeston pointing at his empty plate.

'Yep, Dad's amazing treasure story did the trick,' fibbed Xander.

After helping to wash the dishes, he announced, 'I'm going for a walk to clear my head. Back in twenty minutes or so.'

With that he slipped outside carrying an old blanket he had swiped from the closet. He raced back to footbridge with his fingers crossed all the way. *Please be there. Please be there,* he thought as he sprinted. As soon as he arrived, he peered into the darkness.

'Shiver?'

A friendly bark told Xander his friend had not run away, and he hurried under the bridge. Once his eyes adjusted to the light he spotted Shiver lying on the ground. He was still shivering.

'Hey boy, look what I've got for you,' he said, and held out the lamb. The dog gratefully wolfed it down.

As Xander stroked Shiver's head, he screwed up his nose.

'Phwoar! Tomorrow I'm giving you a bath!' He placed the blanket over Shiver and snuggled up beside him.

Chapter 3

Xander sighed as he reflected upon his run in with the Bruise Brothers.

'One day I'll stand up to them,' he whispered.

Shiver licked Xander's face then let out a high-pitched whine that seemed to say, '*Sure* you will!'

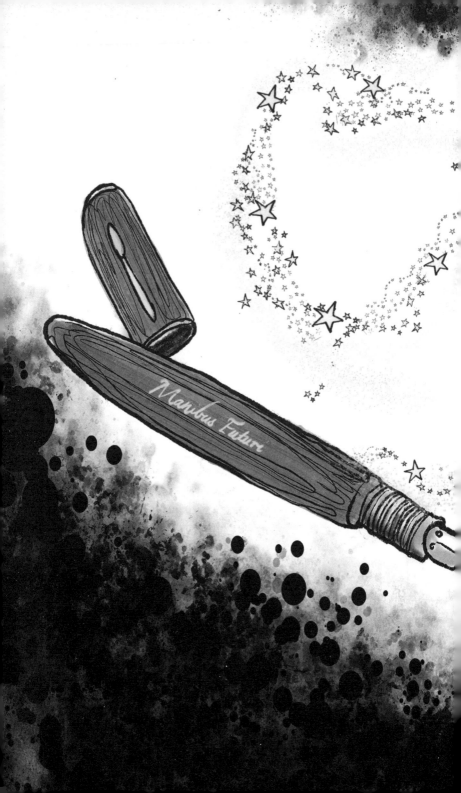

CHAPTER

4

Dark grey storm clouds hung in the air as Xander and his sister set off to school the next morning.

Mr Beeston offered them a lift, but as usual Phoebe declined. 'Xander needs the exercise!' she said.

Phoebe led the way as they headed down the ramp and onto the brick path. She picked up a thin extendable rod from her lap and used it to flick open the catch on the gate. A small shudder went through Xander's body, as he thought back to the day of his sister's bike accident. He remembered the phone ringing, the look on his mother's face and the silence in the car on the way to the hospital.

Phoebe's voice brought him back to the present. 'Hurry up, slowpoke!' she teased.

Xander smiled. He couldn't keep up with his sister even after her accident. Before that terrible day she had been a champion sprinter, and Xander used to call her bedroom a 'museum for blue ribbons'. He jogged to catch up.

'How come we're so different?' Xander asked his sister.

'Well, your hair makes you look like a greyhound with an afro, and I like to keep mine short for playing sport ...'

'I'm not talking about our hair!' said Xander.

'Then what?'

After a short pause he said, 'Phoebs, you've never complained once about ...'

'What's the point of complaining?'

Xander shook his head. Even though Phoebe was a year younger, in many ways she was his big sister.

When they arrived at school, Tee-Jay and Cat were waiting for them just inside the gate.

'Hey,' said Tee-Jay. 'Mum told me about your parents.'

Phoebe nodded.

'They've taken it pretty well,' she said.

Xander brushed back his giant mop of hair and added, 'I have a feeling we'll be eating a lot of fish, and Dad will be reading a lot of Harry Potter!'

They all stopped talking as Jeff Clagg came barrelling through the gate. After spotting Xander and Phoebe, an arrogant smirk spread across his face.

'Awww, did someone's parents lose their jobs?' he said in a baby's voice.

'Get lost Clagg,' said Tee-Jay.

'You better shut up, or I'll get my Dad to sack your parents as well!' snarled Jeff.

'How are *you* ever going to get a job, Jeff?' asked Cat.

'Whaddayamean?'

'Well you can't do basic maths, so …'

'Yes I can!'

'Okay, what's nine times seventeen?'

'That's, um, … nine tens are … um, eighty? And then you have to …'

Jeff spun around and Xander watched him discreetly pull something from his pocket.

'Without using your phone!' insisted Cat.

'I wasn't!' said Jeff, replacing his phone and turning back around.

'And your comprehension skills aren't so good either,' said Cat.

'My *what* skills?'

Phoebe burst out laughing, and Jeff's eyes started twitching. Xander remained frozen like a statue as the bully walked towards his sister.

'I wouldn't do that if I were you, Jeffy,' warned Phoebe.

'What are you going to do, roll over me?' teased Jeff.

He grabbed at her wheelchair, but his hand recoiled like

he'd been bitten by a snake.

Phoebe grinned and gave the retractable rod in her hand another 'swish'.

'Owww! You'll pay for that!' shrieked Jeff, running off with tears in his eyes.

'There's plenty more where that came from!' yelled Phoebe.

Xander exhaled. He realized he had not taken a breath from the moment Jeff walked through the gate. His hands were trembling, and he felt sick in the pit of his stomach. He looked at Phoebe, Tee-Jay and Cat in awe. They were fearless, like superheroes.

A high-pitched bell went off, causing a flurry of activity around the school. 'I'd better get to class,' said Phoebe 'See you later.'

As Phoebe wheeled off, Cat turned to Xander and Tee-Jay.

'We've had some problems on the farm — two of our alpacas died yesterday.'

'How?' asked Xander.

'We think it was something they ate or drank, but we're not sure.'

'If your water was polluted, maybe Clagg's Cannery is to blame,' suggested Tee-Jay. 'They use heaps of chemicals at the factory.'

'Can we come out after school and take a look, Cat?' asked

Xander.

'That'd be really cool — thanks.'

The Cruzes' alpaca farm was only a short ride from Dukescliff. Xander raced home after school to grab his bike so that he and Tee-Jay could go out there together. He hastily threw a water bottle and his sketch pad into a backpack, and headed out the door.

He enjoyed riding and occasionally stayed up late to watch a famous cycling race called the Tour de France with Phoebe and his dad. He loved listening to the commentators trying to make the most boring parts of the race sound interesting. On the way out to Cat's place, Xander decided to entertain Tee-Jay with his own Tour de France-style commentary, using a funny French accent.

'And leading ze peloton in ze yellow jersey, is cycling superstar, Xander "Ze Beast" Beeston!'

Tee-Jay let out a snort.

'And drafting illegally behind him iz his trusty "domestique", Tejas "Tee-Jay" Sah!'

'Domestique?'

'Oui! A domestique iz a rider with zero talent, who iz merely there to protect superstars like … Ze Beast …'

'Hey wait a minute!' complained Tee-Jay.

'And look at zat beautiful blade of grass in ze paddock on ze left! Magnifique! I've never seen a blade of grass quite like it — ooh la la! I can see why so many tourists come down zis way. And vot is zat? Oh my goodness, a tree! A-mazing!'

Tee-Jay laughed as he sped past Xander.

'Let's see if Ze Beast can catch his own domestique!' he called out.

'Oh no! An attack from iz own team! Sacre bleu!'

The Cruzes' dirt driveway had rows of giant pine trees along either side. Xander always felt like he was in a long dark tunnel, and was relieved when he made it to the end. Cat greeted them out the front of the ramshackle farmhouse. Chooks clucked away as they haphazardly roamed the yard, and Xander noted the impressive vegetable garden that ran along the side of the house.

'Mum said to give you some carrots and beetroots before you go,' said Cat.

'Thanks,' said Xander.

He and Tee-Jay wheeled their bikes over to an old run-down wooden garage. They propped them against a wall as Cat started up a small red motorbike with a mighty roar. Xander jumped on behind her while Tee-Jay hopped on a bigger blue bike and brought it growling to life.

'Let's go to the bottom paddock,' yelled Cat.

All three knew the drill, as they had done this many times. As always, the red bike led the way with Tee-Jay struggling to keep up, while a petrified Xander hung onto Cat with all his might.

'I need to be able to breathe!' she laughed.

Whenever they arrived at a gate, it was Xander's job to open it. He would wait until the two bikes went through before shutting it securely. He always made sure to close the gates properly, as he didn't want any of the alpacas to escape. Not only were alpacas expensive to replace, but the Cruzes treated them like they were part of the family.

All the alpacas had nicknames, and because the Cruzes were from Peru, most of these were in Spanish.

'Which alpacas died?' shouted Xander.

As Cat turned around to answer, he could see there were tears in her eyes.

'Hola and Gracias died yesterday. And I just found out we lost Salud today.'

After Xander let them into the bottom paddock, Cat sped over to the large dam that backed onto thick bushland. They hopped off the bikes and Cat pointed to a spot next to the dam.

'That's where we found Hola and Gracias … and Salud

was just near those bushes.'

Tee-Jay stared at the large pool of brown water. 'The cannery is the only factory within fifty kilometres,' he said. 'Do you think it somehow polluted your dam?'

'We *thought* so. But Dad had a water sample checked by the water authority, and it was fine.'

'Maybe there's a clue somewhere else in the paddock?' suggested Tee-Jay.

'Okay, let's split up,' said Cat. 'Xander, how about you look in the bush here, while Tee-Jay and I use the bikes to check the rest of the paddock?'

'No worries,' said Xander.

As the motorbikes started up, he headed into the thick vegetation. It was hard work hacking through the dense shrubs, and after ten minutes he was dripping with sweat. He took off his backpack, sat down on a log and pulled out his drink bottle. In his hurry to leave the house he had only half filled it, so he managed to drink the entire contents in three giant gulps.

'Ahhhhh!' Xander returned the water bottle to the backpack, pulled out his sketch pad and grabbed his pencil from behind his ear. The unexplained alpaca deaths had given him an idea for a new superhero called 'The Shepherd'. He drew a strong, bearded man in a robe holding a stick with a curved end. From the stick came a lightning bolt that was heading towards two evil-looking rustlers who were loading sheep onto the back of a van. The Shepherd's speech bubble said, 'Put those baaaaaaa-ck!'

Xander smiled at his new creation, but as he went to put it away he accidentally knocked his backpack off the back of the log. He leant over to retrieve it and instantly said, 'Phew!' Had the backpack landed a fraction to the right it would have ended up in a large puddle. As Xander picked it up, he noticed that the surface of the puddle had a rainbow-coloured sheen on it. Intrigued, he took out his water bottle, uncapped the lid and bent down to swipe a sample of the water. He stopped momentarily and sniffed the air. *Rotten eggs?*

As he carefully screwed the cap back on, he noticed something moving towards him out the corner of his eye. He leapt back over to the other side of the log as a black snake reared up to reveal its red belly.

'Argh!' he cried. Xander quickly threw the water bottle into his pack and raced through the scrub. Eventually he burst out of the bush and saw Cat and Tee-Jay standing next to the dam.

'Snake!' he yelled. 'Giant snake!'

He raced over to his friends, who studied him with puzzled expressions.

'Calm down, mate,' said Cat. 'It's not chasing you anymore.'

'Yeah, the snake would be more scared of you than you are of it,' added Tee-Jay.

Xander was shaking uncontrollably and opened his mouth, but no words came out.

'Actually, I don't think that's possible.' said Cat. 'How about I see if Dad can give you both a lift home in the van, so you can put your bikes in the back?'

'Th-th-thanks C-c-cat,' stammered Xander.

Xander took some deep breaths as he lay on his bed before dinner that evening. While reliving the deadly snake's attack, he suddenly remembered the water bottle in his backpack and jumped up to inspect it.

He opened his cupboard and found an old science kit his grandfather had given him for Christmas a few years ago. After selecting a test tube from the box, he filled it with some of the murky water he had collected. As he was holding the test tube up to the light, there was a knock at the door and Phoebe wheeled in.

'Dinner time, Xander … hey, what are you up to?'

'Some of the Cruzes' alpacas died and Tee-Jay and I are helping Cat find out what's going on.'

'Good on you,' said Phoebe.

'Yeah, we think Clagg's Cannery might be involved, but we need to be able to prove it.'

'Shame I can't help you with the leg work,' joked Phoebe. 'But how about I do some research?'

'Thanks Phoebs, that'd be great.'

After a lovely dinner of fresh whiting, with carrots and beetroots from the Cruzes' farm, Xander popped into the toilet next to his bedroom. He was about to undo his fly when a golden flash came up from the bowl in front of him.

He peered into the toilet and his eyes widened.

'No way!' he exclaimed in disbelief. He reached into the water and fished out a full bottle of blue ink. Then he reached down again, this time retrieving his special old pen.

As soon as it was in his hand he felt a wonderful warm glow spreading throughout his body.

'Nothing can harm me,' he whispered.

The next thing Xander knew, he was sitting in his bedroom and his mother was knocking on the door.

'Time to go to sleep honey,' she called out.

'But Mum it's only …' Xander looked at his watch and gave it a shake. '… 9.30 p.m.?'

Wheelchair Woman to the Rescue!

'That's right — you should be sound asleep.'

Xander's heart started pounding as he looked down at his desk. The pen was sitting next to a brand-new ink drawing. It was definitely his style … but he could not remember sketching it. It featured a short-haired girl wearing a superhero type outfit with WW on her chest, sitting in a hotted-up wheelchair with flames coming off the wheels. At the bottom of the sketch were the words, 'Wheelchair Woman to the Rescue!'

Xander stared at the superhero in the drawing. *Phoebe?*

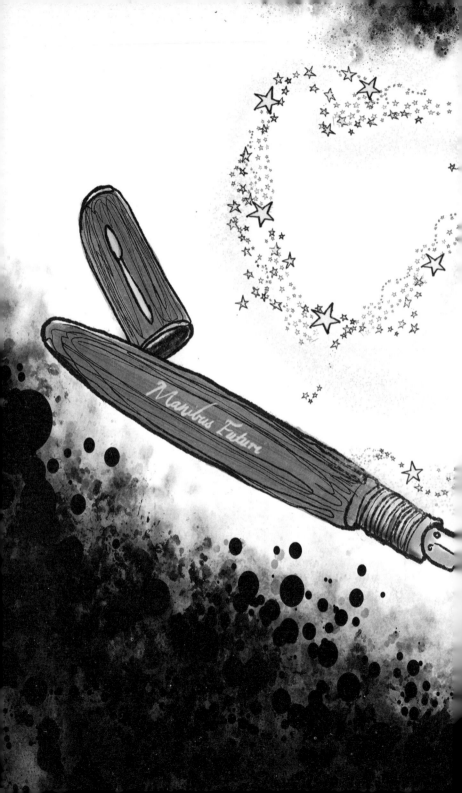

CHAPTER

5

On the way to school the next day, Xander started whistling.

'Someone's in a good mood,' said Phoebe.

'How about we go down Main Street and check out the shops before school?' suggested Xander.

'Okay,' said Phoebe. 'Coz there's *so* many shops!'

They turned left and headed towards the only two shops that were open: the Dukescliff newsagency and Neryl's Café.

Neryl's Café was owned by a man called Barry, but no one cared that his name wasn't Neryl because he made excellent coffees. Xander could see people milling around in front of Neryl's, including a young woman with a pram.

As they approached the café, he heard a booming voice from inside yell, 'Number twenty-four!'

'That's me!' said the woman, leaving her pram as she ducked inside. The pram slowly started rolling down the incline of the footpath. It picked up speed as it went over the curb, heading directly into the path of a speeding four-wheel-drive vehicle.

Xander held his breath and looked away. He heard the screeching of brakes and waited for the sound of the car hitting the pram. *Thump!*

'That poor little baby,' he whispered.

Xander opened his eyes and then rubbed them to make sure he wasn't seeing things. The pram was a crumpled wreck in front of the stationary four-wheel drive, but on the other side of the road was Phoebe in her wheelchair, with the baby in her arms.

The mother ran out of Neryl's in tears, and Phoebe handed her the child.

'Thank you, thank you!' she cried.

Xander rushed over to his sister.

'You okay?'

'Yeah … I think so.'

The driver slowly emerged from his vehicle, looking like he'd seen a ghost.

'S-s-sorry,' he said.

A small crowd gathered and began talking about what they had witnessed.

'How did she do that?'

'I swear it was a blur!'

'She saved that baby's life!'

The approaching sound of a police siren caused the gossiping group to fall silent and take a few steps back.

Moments later, Senior Sergeant Dawson jumped out of her car and calmly walked over to assess the situation.

'Is anyone injured?' she asked.

The driver, the mother and Phoebe all shook their heads.

'We're all okay, officer,' said the driver.

'Thanks to this amazing girl,' said the mother.

'She's a hero,' said an elderly lady. 'A superhero!'

'Well, the community owes you our gratitude,' said the police officer. 'You're Phoebe Beeston, aren't you?'

'Yes.'

'Sounds like you did something incredibly brave — can you talk me through what happened?'

'I'm not really sure; it all happened so fast. I saw the pram rolling towards the street …'

'That was my fault,' said the mother. 'I didn't put the brake on when I went to grab my cappuccino.' Senior Sergeant Dawson frowned then nodded for Phoebe to continue.

'… and I saw the car was going really fast and about to hit the pram …'

'For the record, I definitely wasn't speeding,' interrupted the driver.

The policewoman looked at the skid marks on the road and rolled her eyes. She then turned back to Phoebe.

'Where were you at this stage?'

Phoebe pointed to the footpath on the other side of the road. 'Um, over there somewhere,' she said.

The police officer looked surprised. 'You sure? That's a long way away.'

'It's true, I was standing next to her,' said Xander.

The policewoman looked totally confused.

'So you wheeled your chair all that way, and grabbed the baby before a speeding car crushed the pram?'

'Um, I guess so,' said Phoebe.

'As I said, I wasn't speeding ...'

Senior Sergeant Dawson's stern expression stopped the driver mid-sentence, just as a well-dressed man with a camera pushed his way through the crowd.

'Hey, Dana. Once you're finished asking questions, can I get a few snaps for the newspaper?'

'Knock yourself out, Lenny. Nobody was hurt — luckily!' she said, glaring at the driver. The journalist immediately started taking photos of Phoebe.

'Can we have one of you holding the baby?' he asked, and the mother obligingly handed the baby back to Phoebe. 'Yeah, that's perfect.'

Xander gave his sister an encouraging thumbs up.

'You're a legend, Phoebs!' he whispered.

When Xander arrived home after school he rushed to his bedroom and tossed his school bag in the corner. He couldn't wait to tell his parents about Phoebe's heroics. As he was leaving the room he glanced towards his desk and stopped. He walked over, picked up the ink drawing and read out the caption: 'Wheelchair Woman to the Rescue!'

He pursed his lips and narrowed his gaze. It definitely looked like Phoebe, and the flames coming off the tyres suggested she could move really fast … *Nah — total coincidence.*

'Knock, knock!' called out Phoebe.

Xander wasn't sure why, but he instinctively shoved the sketch into a drawer.

'Come in.'

As his sister wheeled into his room, Xander pretended to make an announcement on a microphone.

'And the "Dukescliff Citizen of the Year" is … just have to open the envelope … oooh, it's our youngest ever winner, will you please make a lot of noise for … Phoebe Beeston!'

'Shut up, Xander! It was no big deal,' laughed Phoebe.

'Tell that to the mother! At one stage I thought she was

going to give you her baby as a reward!'

Phoebe snorted then the smile quickly left her face.

'Hey, I need to be serious for a second,' she said.

'What's up?' asked Xander.

'A couple of Year 4 kids told me Jeff and Tony are planning to get you at lunchtime tomorrow.'

'How come?'

'Apparently you broke the Bruise Brothers code when you dobbed them in to Mum and Dad.'

'The Bruise Brothers have a code?' said Xander.

'Apparently! Anyway, just letting you know in case you want to pretend to be sick tomorrow.'

'Thanks, Phoebs,' replied Xander.

After his sister left, Xander looked down at his trembling hands. *What are they going to do me? The Hedge of Darkness? The Sand Wedgie? Maybe the Sock and Roll … whatever that is?*

Without realizing it, he picked up the pen from the table. A soothing warmth spread throughout his body, and his hands stopped shaking. He even began to smile.

'Nothing can harm me,' he whispered.

Xander guessed he must have dozed off, as the next thing he knew his mother was calling out to him.

'Dinner time, Xander — guess what, we're having fish!'

He smiled and was about to stand up when he noticed a new ink drawing sitting on his desk. Once again he could not remember sketching it. The cartoon depicted a muscly superhero called 'The Ninja Beast' standing triumphantly over the unconscious Clagg brothers. They were wearing T-shirts that read, 'Bruise Bros #1' and 'Bruise Bros #2', and their heads were covered in band-aids. The superhero had his hands on his hips, and his speech bubble said, 'More like the *Bruised* Brothers!'

While the Ninja Beast's body didn't resemble Xander's, his wild hair was unmistakeably the same. Xander smiled, slipped the pen into his pocket and starting whistling.

Just before lunchtime in maths class the next day, Mr Steele's phone started vibrating on his desk. He frowned, picked it up and began reading a text message. He twirled the tip of his moustache and then addressed the class.

'A package has just arrived for me at reception, so while I'm finding out what it is ... Tejas, you're in charge.'

Mr Steele strode from room and the students turned to look at Tee-Jay for direction.

'I don't know ... just do whatever you were doing!' he said.

The door of the classroom opened again, and Xander

assumed that Mr Steele had forgotten something.

But to his surprise the Clagg brothers were standing in the doorway.

'Beast, you're coming with us,' declared Tony.

'Don't go,' said Cat, gripping her friend's arm.

'No, it's fine.'

Cat frowned. 'You sure?'

Xander nodded and strolled confidently towards the doorway.

Once outside he looked both brothers in the eye.

'The oval, boys? Let's go.'

The Bruise Brothers turned to look at each other.

'What's going on?' mouthed Jeff.

'Dunno,' whispered Tony.

'Hey, nice touch with the delivery for Mr Steele,' said Xander. 'I assume that was your idea, Tony?'

'Yeah, but I wrapped the box!' said Jeff. Tony rolled his eyes.

'We wanted to do this *before* lunch, so there were no witnesses,' he said.

'Ingenious,' said Xander. He put his hand in his pocket and felt a surge of energy leap from the pen. Despite being led to the oval by two brutal bullies, he had never felt so calm in all his life.

They stopped when they reached the middle of the ground,

which was quite muddy as a result of some overnight rain.

'Okay, Beast are you ready?' asked Tony.

'It's not "Beast", replied Xander, 'It's *Ninja* Beast!'

He then started making a series of high-pitched squeals as he moved his arms around like he was a martial arts expert.

The Bruise Brothers' faces went bright red and Jeff screamed, 'Let's get him!' Xander continued to make weird noises as the Claggs rushed towards him from different directions.

Just before they got to him, Tony slipped in the mud. *Bang!* His forehead accidentally crashed into Jeff's eye, and they fell to the ground like they'd been struck by lightning — just as the bell went for lunch.

Kids streamed out of classes from everywhere, and most of them headed for the oval. Cat, Tee-Jay and Phoebe were three of the first to arrive and what they saw left them speechless.

Xander was standing over the Clagg boys, who were both dazed and confused. Tony had a giant bump on his forehead and Jeff sported a nasty black eye.

'Bruise Brothers?' said Xander folding his arms, 'More like the *bruised* brothers!'

All the students burst out laughing, which woke up the Claggs.

'Wh-what hit me?' asked Tony.

Jeff's bottom lip was trembling.

'Dunno. What hit *me*?'

They both looked up to see a hundred kids laughing at them, and tried to run away. But the knocks to their heads had made them so dizzy that they kept falling over as if they were on an ice-skating rink.

'How did you do it, Xander?' asked Cat.

'They don't call me the Ninja Beast for nothing.'

'Absolutely *no one* calls you the Ninja Beast!' said Tee-Jay.

Xander laughed and started doing some bizarre martial arts

'Hey, Ninja Beast, can you teach me how do a karate kick?' asked a Year 2 boy.

Xander looked at Tee-Jay. 'See — I am da Ninja Beast!'

That evening, Xander went to visit Shiver. He stuffed half a sandwich left over from lunch into his pocket, and swiped a slice of cheese from the fridge.

Just as he was leaving home he bumped into Phoebe, who was coming up the ramp.

'Hey Phoebs,' he said.

'Hey Xander, or should I say "Ninja Beast"?'

'Xander's fine,' he said with a grin.

'Just wanted to say how proud I am that you stood up to the Claggs today.'

Xander wanted to tell his sister about the pen and the magical drawings, but he wasn't sure he even believed it himself.

'Um, thanks sis — that means a lot to me.'

He started whistling and on his way to the footbridge put his hand in his pocket to feel the reassuring warmth from his pen.

When he arrived, Shiver was waiting in his usual spot.

'Hey boy,' said Xander.

He held up the sandwich and slice of cheese, and they were quickly devoured amidst grateful whines.

Xander then sat down and gave Shiver a hug, before pulling out the pen. He held it up and smiled.

'Everyone seems to like the new Xander …' The dog suddenly started growling at the pen and backing away. '… except Shiver!'

CHAPTER

6

Xander was washing his hands for dinner when he heard a booming knock on the front door.

'Cam, get out here now! And I mean *right* now!' screamed Mr Clagg.

Xander raced to the front of the house and peeked out a window. A red-faced Mr Clagg was now standing in the middle of the front yard. His arms were folded and a giant vein on his left temple looked ready to explode.

Xander sprinted back down the hallway, nearly colliding with his father. Mr Beeston was sweating profusely and looked pale.

'You okay, Dad?'

'I'm fine son. You stay here.'

As his father headed for the door, Xander sprinted to his bedroom. He went to his desk, pulled out a piece of paper and picked up his special pen. Straight away he felt calm, strong and in control. A smile appeared on his face as he started scribbling.

'How dare your son beat up my sons!' yelled Mr Clagg.

'From what I hear, your sons were trying to beat up my son, and …'

As the two men argued, Xander finished off his drawing with the caption, 'David versus Goliath'. It showed a small balding man, resembling his father, conquering a very embarrassed-looking giant who looked like Mr Clagg.

Xander rushed back to the front of the house, hoping his drawing would work. He peered out the window just as Mr Clagg whipped the belt off his trousers.

'Time to give you a *belt*ing, Cam!'

Unfortunately his trousers fell down straight away, revealing a pair of silky Scooby Doo boxer shorts. The Quarry Street neighbours, who were looking on, all burst out laughing.

'Scooby Doooooo!' howled Mr Lee.

'Who let the dogs out!' yelled Mrs McNamara.

These comments made Mr Clagg even angrier. He charged forward, but fell flat on his face because his trousers were around his ankles. The spectators all roared with laughter again.

'Hope you enjoyed your *trip*!' yelled Mr Lee.

'Best face plant ever!' said Mrs McNamara.

'That is *it*!' screamed Mr Clagg. He pulled up his pants and approached Mr Beeston while threatening him with his belt. In response, Mr Beeston picked up a hose with a sprinkler attached to it and started waving it above his head like a lasso. Xander thought this was a clever move, because it prevented Mr Clagg from getting too close.

'I can do this all day, Tristan,' said Mr Beeston. 'So go home and we can talk over the phone when you've cooled down.'

Suddenly the sprinkler became disconnected from the hose and flew directly into Mr Clagg's head. He shrieked and fell to the ground.

'Hey Cam, I hope your sprinkler's okay!' called out Mrs McNamara.

Clutching at his beltless trousers, Mr Clagg jumped up and headed back to his sports car parked in the street.

'You haven't heard the last of this!' he yelled. As he walked around the back of his car, his shin collided with the tow bar.

'Aaaaaaghhh!'

With tears in his eyes, and his pants around his ankles, Mr Clagg crawled into his car then sped off to the raucous applause of the Quarry Street residents.

Inside the house Xander grinned as he pulled the pen from his pocket.

'You are *awesome!*' he whispered.

That night at dinner everyone was in a good mood, and Xander held up his fork with a piece of whiting on it.

'Dad, you obviously caught some fish today, but what we *really* want to know is … did you read any Harry Potter?'

'Harry who?' said Mr Beeston.

'Come on Dad, we know you're a closet fan,' said Phoebe.

'I have no idea what you're talking about, and if you don't stop, I'll put an Imperius curse on both of you!'

'That's pathetic, Dad!' laughed Xander.

'Now, now. Don't make fun of your father,' said Mrs Beeston with a straight face. 'So Cam, did you manage to find Finito's treasure today?' Xander and Phoebe both snorted.

'Not today, Betty … but I did find some amazing bottle tops!'

'Bottle tops are pretty lame, but facing up to Mr Clagg was really cool,' said Xander.

'Oh, I don't know … actually, I was pretty cool, wasn't I?' said Mr Beeston.

'Did you see the look on his face when his trousers fell

down?' laughed Phoebe.

'Shcooby Roo!' said Xander.

The sound of the phone interrupted the family banter.

'I'll get it,' said Mr Beeston.

'It's probably an agent wanting to book you for an MMA fight,' suggested Xander.

'Or J.K. Rowling wanting some advice on a new storyline,' said Phoebe.

Mr Beeston casually picked up the phone attached to the wall near the kitchen.

'Yell-ow … Hey Dana, what's up? … What? … I appreciate you not coming to the house … yep, I'll be there in fifteen minutes.'

Mr Beeston hung up the phone, and slowly walked back to the table.

'That was Senior Sergeant Dawson … I have to go down to the police station.'

'How come?' asked Mrs Beeston.

'She said an assault charge has been filed against me: "Intention to harm with a deadly weapon".'

'Deadly weapon? It was a sprinkler!' said Xander.

'And he was attacking *you* with his belt!' said Phoebe.

'Yeah, but Mr Clagg was the one who was injured,' explained Mr Beeston.

'How can Dana do this? She knows what Tristan's like,' said Mrs Beeston.

'She's only doing her job, honey. She could have arrested me in front of everyone, but she's letting me turn myself in.'

Mr Beeston headed to the hallway to grab his coat from the hook, and Mrs Beeston leapt up from the table to follow him.

As his parents started their private conversation, Xander strained his ears to listen in.

'... but you didn't do anything wrong,' whispered Mrs Beeston.

'I'll be fine. The only thing that worries me is the cost.'

'The cost?'

'Lawyers. I'll need to hire one to defend this stupid charge ,and Dana said Tristan mentioned suing me for hundreds of thousands of dollars ... and you know he'll hire the best lawyers that money can buy.'

'Cam, we don't have jobs, and with Phoebe's medical bills ...' Mrs Beeston started sobbing quietly.

'Hey, look at me,' said Mr Beeston. 'We always land on our feet, don't we?'

'Yep,' said Mrs Beeston, wiping away her tears. 'Maybe you'll find Finito's treasure!'

They both had a chuckle and then Xander heard the front

door opening and closing.

He pulled the pen from his pocket and stared at it.

'What's that?' asked Phoebe.

'I thought it was my lucky pen … now I'm not so sure.'

CHAPTER

7

As Xander arrived at school the next day, he spotted a young, bearded groundsman working on the oval.

'What's he doing, Phoebs?' asked Xander.

'Marking the running lanes for Friday's house athletics.'

'Oh, of course … sorry.'

'That's cool. It'll be different this year, but I'll be fine.'

Xander felt sick. *And the award for 'Worst Brother Ever' goes to … me!* He spent the rest of the day trying to imagine how it would feel for a champion sprinter to be told they would never walk, let alone run again. The thought of Phoebe sitting in her wheelchair watching the other kids compete made him sad.

After tossing and turning in bed that night, his eyes suddenly opened. He leapt out of bed, flicked on the desk lamp and grabbed a sheet of paper from a drawer. He then picked up his beautiful old pen, and as its soothing warm energy spread throughout his body he started drawing.

When he had finished his cartoon he put down his pen and studied it closely. A superhero called 'The Healer' was shooting light from her eyes into the legs of a short-haired girl in a wheelchair. The girl was smiling, and The Healer's speaking bubble said, 'Arise!' Xander placed the cartoon in a drawer, jumped back into bed and went into a deep, deep sleep …

At 6.30 a.m. the next morning, he was woken by a high-pitched squeal.

He followed the shouts of excitement to the kitchen, where his mum was jumping up and down. Standing next to Mrs Beeston was Phoebe. *Standing!*

'No way!' said Mr Beeston rushing past Xander to give his daughter a hug.

'H-h-how?'

'No idea! I woke up and had this tingling feeling in my legs and …' Phoebe did a little dance, finishing with a twirl, before looking over at Xander.

'You don't seem surprised?'

'I'm just happy for you, sis … think you'll be able to walk to school today?'

'Walk? No way! We're *running* to school!'

'Uh, uh,' said Mrs Beeston. 'I'm taking you straight to the

specialist to find out what's going on.'

'But *Mum!*'

'No buts — we need to check everything so you don't have a relapse. Okay?'

'Okay,' grumbled Phoebe.

It was a perfect Friday afternoon featuring a cloudless blue sky with barely a breath of wind. The smell of freshly cut grass hung in the air as the sounds of cheering students competed with announcements over the PA system, and the intermittent blast of the starter's pistol.

Everyone was dressed in one of the four house colours: red for Newton, blue for Goodall, yellow for Curie, and green for Hawking.

The school's principal, Mr Whisker, had arrived two years ago, and one of his first actions was renaming the houses after famous scientists. He hoped this would stimulate the students' interest in science and lift the school's rather average academic results. He'd been dismayed to discover that according to Wikipedia, the school's two most notable ex-students were a progressive house DJ living in Ibiza, and a reality TV cooking show runner-up from 2011.

Xander spotted Phoebe talking to the sports coach, Mrs

Faletta, near the start for the 100-metre sprint. He rushed over to wish her good luck, and noticed that Mrs Faletta was frowning.

'Phoebe, are you *sure* you're allowed to compete?'

'Yes! The X-rays prove I'm 100 per cent okay, and the doctors gave me the all clear.'

'Doctors! Pfft,' said Mrs Faletta. She rolled her eyes and stomped off.

'Doctors! Pfft,' said Xander. 'Sure they're really smart and they study super hard for years, but *what* would they know?'

'Yeah, what would doctors know about … medicine!' laughed Phoebe.

'Just wanted to say best of luck, but don't push it too hard,' said Xander.

'*You* are giving *me* athletics advice, bro?'

'Mmm, that doesn't sound right does it?'

'Don't worry — I'm just happy to be running again.'

Xander put his hand in his pocket and felt the warmth emanating from his pen.

'We're happy too.'

'*We're* happy?' said Phoebe.

'Um, I meant, um, we as in … Mum, Dad and me.'

Their conversation was interrupted by an announcement over the PA system.

'Will the starters for girls' under-twelve, 100 metre sprint please take your lanes?'

'Better go,' said Phoebe.

Xander dashed off to find a good vantage point, but discovered this was an impossible task. Everyone wanted to watch Phoebe's comeback run, and all Xander could see was the back of people's heads.

'Over here!' yelled a familiar voice. Xander bolted over to Tee-Jay, who helped him up onto his shoulders. Instantly he had a perfect view of the track. A tense silence was broken by the starter's voice.

'On your marks ... get set ...' *Bang!*

Xander watched Phoebe burst out of the blocks, quickly taking a huge lead over the other runners. That gap seemed to grow exponentially as she powered down the track. The announcer was so excited that Xander feared he might suffer a heart attack.

'... Phoebe Beeston is absolutely flying, she's like a yellow blur, I've never seen anything like this, OMG, this is amazing, look at her go, come on Phoebe! Go! Yesssss — she breaks the tape with no one near her! This is *unbelievable*, I cannot wait to see her time! And if I accidentally swore during that race call, I apologize. Actually, who cares if I did? That was the most freakish run I've ever seen — Curie

House should get bonus points …'

All the students were jumping up and down; some of the teachers too! Xander even spotted Mr Whisker doing a quiet fist pump.

'… and I have just been given Phoebe Beeston's time for the 100 metres,' said the announcer.

Everyone went quiet.

'… 11.99 seconds! That is a new world record for an eleven-year-old — Phoebe Beeston you are an absolute star!'

Xander walked into the kitchen the next morning, to find his parents and Phoebe flicking through a pile of newspapers.

'Your sister's on the front page!' said Mr Beeston. 'And not just the local papers!'

Xander rushed over and read a few of the headlines.

'Miracle Girl Smashes World Record!'

'The Queen of Dukescliff!'

'Flying Phoebe on Top of the World!'

One national newspaper had a photo of Phoebe in her wheelchair next to one of her crossing the finishing line. It was accompanied by the heading: 'Chairway to Heaven!'

'This is amazing,' said Xander picking up the local news-paper. 'Oh, check this out Phoebs, they interviewed Mrs

THE
LATEST
NEWS
☆ & ☆
PICTURES

VOL XXI No 11

Morr

HERA

Chairway t

School coach
success!!!

Acclaimed school sports coach Mrs Faletta proudly explained yesterday how she was the only one who convinced the 11 year old star to race. "I looked her straight in the eye and I said don't worry about what the doctors say, I want you to run!"

11 year
the

ng

LD

DAILY
Newspaper
⚜ $1 ⚜

SPECIAL EDITION

Heaven!

NISH

tar defies
to win

World Record Smashed

The world U/12 100 metre record was smashed yesterday by elite Dukesliffe High student Phoebe Beeston who miracously overcame a crippling illness to beat all the competitors and set a new time of 11.99 seconds.

Faletta!'

'What did she say?'

'Sports coach Veronica Faletta said she had to convince the eleven-year-old star to race. 'I looked Phoebe in the eye and said, "Don't worry about what the doctors say, I want you to run!"'

'OMG!' said Phoebe.

They were interrupted by the sound of the phone.

'Hey, let Phoebe get it — I'm sure they want to speak to the Queen of Dukescliff!' said Xander. Phoebe poked out her tongue and raced over to answer it.

'Hello, Phoebe speaking … yes, of course I remember you … really? … oh definitely … when? … Wow, thank you, thank you so much ... yep, I'll talk to my parents … bye.'

Phoebe hung up and let out such a high-pitched squeal that Xander wondered if all the windows would shatter.

'I'm guessing that was *good* news,' said Mr Beeston.

'That was the headmistress of Riverview Girls Grammar and …'

'And?' asked Mrs Beeston

'The offer for a full scholarship is back on!'

This time Mrs Beeston let out a high-pitched scream.

'That's great news, honey — do you start next year?' she asked.

'No … in two weeks' time!'

'Two weeks? That's … really soon,' said Xander.

'That's okay, right?'

'Of course — we'll miss you, that's all,' said Mrs Beeston.

'Speak for yourself, Mum,' said Xander. 'We won't miss Phoebs at all — will we, Dad?'

'That's right son — probably won't even notice she's gone!'

'Aww Dad, is that a tear in your eye?' asked Phoebe.

'No, no … just a bit of hay fever,' sniffed Mr Beeston. 'In fact, I'd better grab a tablet.'

As Mr Beeston rushed out of the room, Xander noticed that Mrs Beeston was also crying. But it was when he felt a tear rolling down his own cheek that he realized how different things would be without his sister around.

The next morning the school was buzzing with talk about Phoebe's stunning race.

'I would take the credit,' joked Xander, 'but Mrs Faletta beat me to it!'

He was standing under the giant Monterey cypress tree with Cat and Tee-Jay, who both laughed.

Then Tee-Jay turned to Cat and said, 'Are you going to tell him or will I?'

'What gives?' asked Xander.

'We found more dead animals on the farm yesterday,' explained Cat. 'A couple of birds and a red bellied black snake.'

Xander shuddered. 'That must have been the giant one that attacked me!' he said.

Cat held up her hands a short distance apart. 'It was *this* big!'

Xander's face went the colour of the snake's belly.

'Okay, okay — can we move on with the story?' he said.

'Last night Cat and I snuck out to the cannery,' said Tee-Jay. 'To see if any of their chemicals might be poisoning the animals.'

'Why didn't you ask me to come along?'

Cat and Tee-Jay exchanged a quick glance.

'We thought you might freak out ...' started Cat, '... and get us caught,' finished off Tee-Jay.

Xander put his hand in his pocket, and as soon as his fingers touched the pen, he received a jolt of energy. But it felt different. He screwed up his face and clenched his fists.

'I can't believe you guys went without me! Why would I freak out? I'm the one who took down the Bruise Brothers — not you!'

Cat and Tee-Jay stared at him in shocked silence.

'Coz I'm da Ninja Beast,' said Xander. He started making high-pitched noises and doing some ridiculous martial arts moves, causing Cat and Tee-Jay to burst out laughing.

'Gee, you really had me going there,' said Cat.

'We'll make sure we ask you next time — not that there'll be a next time,' said Tee-Jay.

'How come?' asked Xander.

'Because they have a security guard standing at the only entrance.'

'And he looked really mean,' added Tee-Jay.

Cat shook her head.

'There's no way to get past him.'

Xander looked off into the distance over Cygnet Bay. *Unless you were … invisible!*

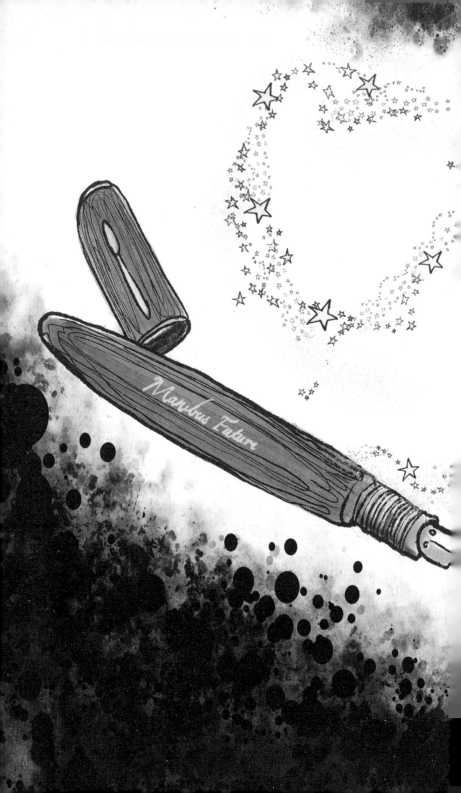

CHAPTER
8

To Xander's surprise, fish was not on the menu for dinner that night.

'We need variety,' announced Mr Beeston. 'That's why we're having … squid!'

'Wow, Dad — for a second there I thought we were going to eat something that *didn't* come from the ocean!'

Ignoring his son's remark, Mr Beeston added, 'And in further good news, The Seeker and I managed to find …'

'Finito's treasure?' said Phoebe.

'… no, this!'

Mr Beeston held up a rusty old metal sign that said 'Dukescliff Petrol'.

There was an awkward silence.

'*So* … what do you think?' pressed Mr Beeston.

Xander pointed to the metal detector in the corner.

'Even The Seeker looks embarrassed about finding *that*!'

Phoebe and Mrs Beeston both snorted.

'It's part of the town's history and it'll scrub up well,' said Mr Beeston defensively.

'Of course it will, honey,' said Mrs Beeston. 'And it'll look great on the wall of the …'

'Lounge room?' said Phoebe.

'Bedroom?' suggested Xander.

'Backyard shed,' finished Mrs Beeston.

Later that evening Xander said good night and went to his bedroom.

He pulled out a piece of paper, then looked around for his special pen. A sudden burst of energy reminded him of where he'd left it — behind his right ear. Xander started drawing a curly-haired superhero called 'Invisible Boy' who was holding a small bottle with 'Invisible Ink' written on it. He added a speech bubble that said, 'Time to go into … *Stealth Mode*!'

After taking a deep breath, he picked up his ink bottle and unscrewed the lid. *Here goes 'nothing'*, he thought.

He tipped some blue liquid onto his hands and rubbed them together. Xander's mouth opened wide as his hands vanished before his eyes.

He lifted the bottle above his head and poured ink onto

his hair. As it trickled down he started rubbing it over his face and clothes. Parts of him disappeared immediately — it was just like using an eraser on a pencil drawing!

Xander smiled as the jar of ink replenished itself whenever it was about to run out. He inspected himself in the mirror above his desk. All he could see were the odd spots he had missed — an elbow, part of his cheek and a small section above his left knee. After dabbing ink onto these areas, he waited until he was sure everyone was asleep. Xander then crept over to his window, undid the latch and pushed up the frame. Then he quietly climbed out and set off down Quarry Street, briefly stopping while Mrs McNamara placed half a dozen empty bottles into a yellow recycling bin.

Later, as he ran past the footbridge, he considered visiting Shiver, before remembering he was invisible. He jogged on and it wasn't long before the Clagg's Cannery sign loomed into view. From outside the fence Xander could see a burly security guard sitting on a chair next to the door that led into the main building. As he crept towards the guard, Mr Clagg suddenly emerged from the factory.

'Oi! What are you doing?' he screamed.

Xander froze. *How can he see me?*

'You call yourself a security guard, Bruno — you were sound asleep!' yelled Mr Clagg.

'I wasn't asleep,' insisted Bruno. 'I was just resting my eyes.'

'Well, you'll have plenty of time to rest them after I fire you!' growled Mr Clagg as he headed towards his sports car.

Xander watched the car speed off, then he walked towards the guard who was muttering to himself. '… thinks he's so special! "Oooh, look at me, I've got a fancy car! I'm the big boss. You're fired!" I'd like to fire *him* …'

Xander took a pebble from his pocket and tossed it so that it landed on the roof to the right of the guard. The big bald-headed man leapt to his feet.

'I-is anybody th-there?' he said uncertainly. He moved towards where the noise had come from, as Xander quietly slipped through the door.

It was pitch black inside, so Xander pulled out a torch and switched it on. 'Invisible Boy activating "Detective Mode",' he whispered.

He wandered around the factory looking for leaky pipes, barrels filled with lethal chemicals, or anything else that might have killed the animals on the Cruzes' farm. After twenty minutes he was about to give up, when his torch caught a glint from an object on the floor near the far wall.

He walked over and found a sturdy padlock attached to a square-shaped trapdoor. Xander bent down and jiggled the padlock. It didn't budge.

Suddenly he heard a car door slam, followed by some yelling.

'Are you asleep again?' screamed Mr Clagg.

'No, I was, um … meditating,' said Bruno. 'Namaste!'

'Don't you "namaste" me … '

Xander's heart was racing as he flicked off his torch. 'Uh oh!' he whispered. Just before the light went out, he had noticed his hand. His hand that he wasn't supposed to notice, because it was supposed to be invisible. Xander rushed to hide behind some barrels that were neatly stacked next to a wall, but his foot clipped the padlock causing him to trip.

The torch fell from his grasp and landed somewhere in the darkness. As Xander frantically groped around for it, he heard Mr Clagg's voice outside the factory.

'What was that?'

Xander leapt to his feet and scrambled towards the barrels. He felt his way around to the back of them and ducked down, just as the door burst open. There was the sound of a switch being flicked, and suddenly the factory floor was awash with light. Xander crouched down even further. He looked through a small crack between two of the barrels and spotted a red-faced Mr Clagg stomping over to the trapdoor and bending down to check the lock.

The factory owner looked around, and suddenly his eyes

widened. He slowly walked over and picked up Xander's torch from the floor.

'Bruno, we have an intruder … lock the door!'

Xander heard the bolt of the factory door sliding shut and started to tremble.

'I know you're in here,' yelled out Mr Clagg.

Xander was shaking so badly he accidentally bumped one of the barrels, causing it to wobble.

'And now I know *exactly* where you are!'

Xander watched as Mr Clagg and Bruno began walking towards him. There was no escape. He couldn't breathe, and his stomach was churning so badly he thought he was going to throw up.

Suddenly Xander felt a surge of energy coming from his right temple. Instinctively he pulled the pen from his sweaty mass of hair, and calmly turned to face the wall. He effortlessly drew a small door with a handle on the bricks, and popped the pen back behind his ear.

His drawing instantly became 3D, and he gratefully turned the handle and scrambled outside. He hurriedly closed his escape hatch then watched the door and handle vanish without a trace. Xander took a deep breath and listened to what was happening on the other side of the wall.

'Gotcha!' screamed Mr Clagg. 'Huh?'

'There's no one here, boss,' said Bruno.

'I can see that, you idiot!' yelled Mr Clagg. 'But there *was* someone snooping around.'

'So, um, what do you want me to do?'

'Double security, set up motion detector alarms, get a guard dog, and throw this torch into the crusher ...'

As Xander listened to the crunching sound of his torch being pulverized, he realized that with the extra security it would now be impossible to sneak into the factory. Even if he was invisible.

Tee-Jay and Cat won't be happy, he thought. *Might be best to keep the Invisible Boy story to myself.*

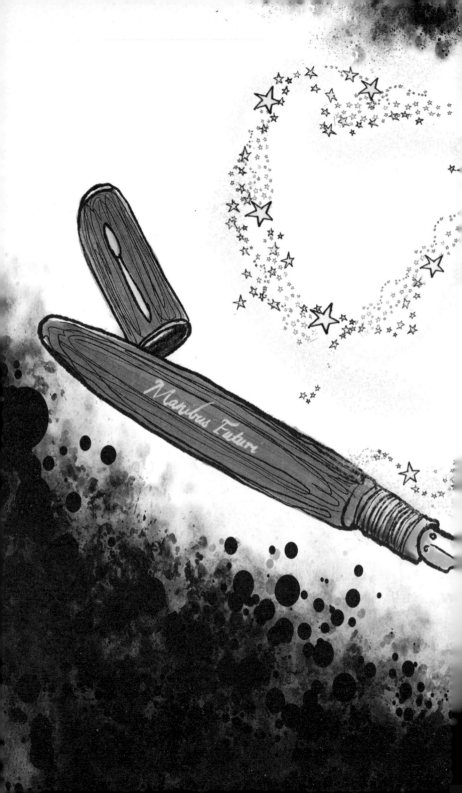

CHAPTER

9

The night before Phoebe left for boarding school, the Beestons held a special farewell dinner.

Mr Beeston had travelled around to Port Gatsby to collect mussels, and traded a large catch of King George whiting with Cat's parents for a leg of lamb.

Mrs Beeston even set the table with the 'nice' dinner plates. These plates had once belonged to her great-grandparents, and only ever came out on important occasions. Xander remembered the last time they had appeared — Grandpa Beeston's 65th birthday. Unfortunately, his tipsy grandfather had accidently chipped a plate while telling an old fishing story. At the time Mrs Beeston laughed it off, but the next day she was furious with her husband, and the nice plates had not been seen since.

'I'd like to propose a toast,' said Xander holding up his glass of water. 'We are going to miss you *so* much … um …

sorry, what was your name again?'

'Very funny!' said Phoebe.

'We'll miss you, honey. But we know it's a great opportunity, and we're really proud,' said Mrs Beeston.

'Felicity?' said Xander. 'No that's not it … it definitely starts with an "f" sound … I want to say, Philippa?'

'Getting closer, bro,' said Phoebe.

'That's enough clowning around, Xander!' said Mr Beeston. 'The Seeker and I have a gift for you, Phoebe.' Mr Beeston handed Phoebe a present that was wrapped in an old newspaper.

'Don't blame The Seeker for the wrapping, that was me,' he explained.

Phoebe opened the gift and her eyes widened. She picked up the necklace then stared in awe at the elegant thin golden chain attached to a white tear-shaped stone.

'It's beautiful!' she said.

'OMG Dad, where did you find that?' asked Xander.

'I didn't really find it — it was your Nanna's,' explained Mr Beeston. 'She wanted Phoebs to have it, and …' He stopped as tears formed in his eyes.

'… we've been waiting for the right time to give it to you,' finished Mrs Beeston.

'I really miss Nanna,' said Phoebe. 'This is … so special.'

Everyone started crying and Xander called out, 'Group hug!'

All four Beestons rose from their seats and put their arms around each other.

Suddenly Xander looked at his sister and said, 'Hey, I just remembered — it's Fifi, right?'-

After dinner Xander went to see Phoebe in her bedroom — a room dominated by blue ribbons and shelves laden with silver trophies. On the bed was an open, neatly packed suitcase, as well as a framed family photograph.

'I'm taking that photo with me,' said Phoebe.

'It's a great one,' said Xander.

He picked up the snapshot and smiled. It included all *five* family members — Mum, Dad, Phoebe, himself and … The Seeker!

'It's great how Dad's holding his favourite child,' he joked. Phoebe rolled her eyes.

'Oops, I nearly forgot!' said Phoebe. 'Meant to give you my research on Clagg's Cannery. Didn't find much, but it's really cool how you and Tee-Jay are helping out Cat's family.'

A feeling of guilt washed over Xander. Since his unsuccessful mission as Invisible Boy, he had barely given the

Cruzes' alpacas a second thought. He watched Phoebe take a manila folder from her desk, then sit down next to him on the bed.

'I went back through the archives at the Dukescliff Historical Centre and found out there used to be a general store where they built the factory.'

Phoebe opened the file and handed Xander a photocopy of the front page of the local newspaper from twenty years ago. There was a photo of a small, square-shaped shop with a petrol pump out the front. Xander smiled and pointed to a sign that said 'Dukescliff Petrol'.

'Now we the know the history of Dad's amazing discovery!' he said. He then started reading the article out loud.

'"Today Paul and Pauline Simmonds say goodbye to their general store after twenty-five years" … hey, I wonder if that's the same Paul Simmonds who lives at the end of Quarry Street?'

'Could be. His wife died a few years ago — that's when Mum started dropping in the odd casserole to help him out.'

Xander nodded.

'Mum does that for a lot of people,' he said.

'Yeah … she did … until she lost her job.'

Xander sighed and returned to reading the article.

'"The couple do not want to stand in the way of the new

canning factory that will employ hundreds of local people and bring enormous economic benefits to Dukescliff. The cannery will be owned and run by respected local businessman Tristan Clagg, who promised the facility would be constructed using 'world's best' environmental practices.'"

Xander screwed up his face. 'Yeah right!' he said.

'And what about "*respected* local businessman"?' added Phoebe.

Xander closed the folder and nervously looked at the floor. He turned to Phoebe.

'Before you go there's something I have to tell you. I've been keeping this secret, and it's going to sound crazy …'

Suddenly the door burst open and Mr Beeston leaned into the room.

'Time for bed, Phoebs — you've got an early start tomorrow.'

'Sure, Dad. Oh, by the way, I left my *Harry Potter and the Deathly Hallows* on your pillow.'

'No way!' gushed a wide-eyed Mr Beeston. 'I've been really wanting to … I mean, "The Deathly" *what*? Haven't heard of it, but you know, if I get time, I might check it out.' He then let out an extremely fake yawn.

'Feeling pretty tired myself. Might turn in about … now. Goodnight!' he said.

Xander listened as his father scampered towards his bed-room, and shook his head.

'Reckon he would have started reading it yet?' he asked.

'He'd be up to page three at least!' said Phoebe. 'Hey, what was the secret you were about to tell me?'

'Oh yeah …'

Xander wanted to tell his sister about the pen, but a sudden burst of energy from behind his ear changed his mind.

'Um, I found a sick dog under the footbridge and I've been sneaking him food. I, um, call him Shiver.'

'That's really cool. But why would I think you're crazy? That's just you being you.'

'I don't know … all I know is I'm going to miss you, sis.'

'Aww,' said Phoebe. 'Remember, I'll be back in six weeks for end of term holidays.'

When Xander woke the next morning, Phoebe was already on her way to boarding school. He guessed she would be fighting over which radio station to listen to in the car, and knew exactly how the conversation with their father would go.

'Phoebs, let's put it on Classic Hits for *one* song, and if you don't like it we'll swap.'

'I hate this song!'

'You can't hate this song — it's a classic! Just wait for the next one, you'll love it!'

'Dad!'

Xander jumped out of bed and headed towards the kitchen. He could hear his mum talking quietly on the phone and stopped to listen in.

'We're struggling to be honest ... losing our jobs has made it tough — we've still got Phoebe's medical bills to pay off, and the mortgage ... but I can't complain, there's lots of people worse off than us ...'

Xander returned to his bedroom, pulled out a piece of paper and grabbed the pen from behind his ear. As a surge of energy raced through his body, his eyes narrowed and a frown appeared on his face. *It's not fair!* he thought. *I helped Phoebs, so why not help Mum and Dad too?*

He drew a picture of a bald-headed, slightly overweight man alongside a curly-haired woman. They were both in superhero outfits outside Clagg's Cannery, which was on fire. The female superhero was blowing out the fire with her icy breath, as the male superhero's speech bubble said, 'We're back to save the day!'

As Xander admired his work, the phone started ringing. He rushed into the hallway to eavesdrop, just as his mum picked up the receiver.

'Hello … what do *you* want? … So, I'd get my old job back? … What about Cam? … Well, it's no deal then … Good! And I want this in writing so you can't fire us again … Okay, I'll be there in an hour … bye.' Mrs Beeston put down the phone and let out a high-pitched squeal.

It's like Phoebe never left! thought Xander as he rushed to the kitchen.

'What's going on?' Xander asked his mum.

'That was Portia Clagg.'

'Why was she calling you?'

'She's the factory's HR manager, and she's giving your dad and me our old jobs back!'

'How come?'

'They had to sack two employees for hacking into the company's computer, and now the whole system needs to be reset. I'm the only one who knows all the passwords, so they can't operate the place without me!'

'But what about Dad?'

'I said it was both of us, or none of us.'

'Great negotiating, Mum!'

'Hey, don't tell your father they only wanted me back — he can get a bit funny about those types of things.'

Xander smiled. 'Don't worry — I can keep a secret.'

At school the next morning, Xander spotted Tee-Jay in the distance.

His shoulders were slumped, his head was down and Cat was giving him a supportive hug.

Xander raced over and said, 'Tee-Jay, whaddup?'

'Mum and Dad ... got fired.'

'No way!' said Xander.

'Mr Clagg accused them of computer hacking and stealing. He even said they broke into the factory a week ago. It's nuts!'

'Can you believe he accused the Sahs of stealing, Xander?' said Cat. 'They're the most honest people in Dukescliff!'

Xander felt nauseous. All he could say was, 'I am so sorry, Tee-Jay.'

'Don't apologize, mate. It's not your fault.'

Xander stared at the ground as he weighed up whether to tell his two best friends about the pen.

'Hey Teej, you have to get your head back in the game,' said Cat. 'We've got that big maths competition this morning.'

'Ohhh, I'd forgotten all about that,' said Xander.

'How could you?' asked Cat. 'Tee-Jay talks about it every

five minutes.'

'So let's not be late!' said Tee-Jay, pointing in the direction of the classroom.

Mr Steele stood in front of the class with a stern look on his face.

He twirled his moustache then cleared his throat to make sure his students were listening.

'Ahem! Principal Whisker has insisted that *all* students enter the National Mathematics Accelerator Competition, not just our gifted ones.'

Mr Steele then did the most exaggerated eye roll Xander had ever seen.

'Anyway,' he continued, 'students who are placed in the top ten nationally will travel to Canberra to meet the country's top professors, who will act as their mentors. The aim is to fast track the mathematical skills of these young geniuses.'

Xander looked across at Tee-Jay and saw him cross his fingers.

'If only this competition had been around when I was at school,' sighed Mr Steele. It was Xander's turn to roll his eyes.

Mr Steele started handing out the test, but stopped at Xander's desk.

'Not sure why I'm giving you this, Beeston. What a complete waste of paper!'

Xander felt a flash of anger course throughout his body and instinctively retrieved his pen from behind his ear.

'I'll show him!' he whispered. He pulled out a sheet of paper and quickly drew a superhero with a mass of curly hair called 'Calculator Boy'. Calculator Boy was arresting an evil, bald-headed man with a curly moustache, who was wearing a lab coat. The superhero's speech bubble said, 'You *calculated* wrong, Professor Steele!'

Xander smiled at his drawing then looked over at Mr Steele.

That should shut him up!

A week after the maths test, the principal announced a special assembly.

Special assemblies were usually only convened if there was bad news. As a result, the teachers and students crammed into the old school hall were feeling anxious. Xander was sitting with Cat and Tee-Jay, as Mr Whisker walked towards the lectern. Everyone fell silent.

'I have some excellent news,' he said.

The audience let out a collective sigh of relief.

'The results of the National Mathematics Accelerator Competition have been released, and one of our students came second in the entire country.'

Xander looked across at Tee-Jay, who was crossing his fingers on both hands.

'This is an extraordinary achievement,' said the principal, 'And when I name this student, I'd like them to stand, so we

can give them a huge round of applause. Congratulations …
Tejas Sah!'

Tee-Jay smiled and jumped to his feet.

The students and teachers all clapped and cheered.

'You da man, Tee-Jay!' yelled Xander.

'You're a legend, Teej!' roared Cat.

Xander looked across at Mr Steele, who smugly raised his
hand to take the credit.

Cat slapped Tee-Jay on the back as he sat down and
Xander watched his friend give an excited fist pump as the
applause petered out.

'But there's more good news,' said the principal. 'Not only
did this school produce the student who came second in the
country, it also produced the student who came first!'

The audience let out an audible gasp. Tee-Jay's smile was
replaced by a look of confusion, and he started nervously
tapping his right foot on the floor.

'So put your hands together for the country's number
one mathematical brain … Xander Beeston!' boomed Mr
Whisker.

There was a delayed reaction from the students. Some of
Xander's classmates even started laughing as they thought
Mr Whisker was joking.

'Stand up *now*, Xander!' ordered the principal.

As he slowly rose to his feet, Xander went bright red and beads of sweat appeared on his forehead. The volume of the applause quickly picked up, and a group of Year 4 kids started chanting, 'Number one! Number one!'

Xander looked at Tee-Jay and Cat. They were clapping, but their eyebrows were raised. He glanced over at Mr Steele, who folded his arms and scowled back at him.

Eventually the applause faded and Xander gratefully sat back down. He turned to Tee-Jay and Cat and shrugged his shoulders, as Mr Whisker started to speak again.

'To have the top two mathematical students in the country at such a small school is remarkable. The only sad news is the rules only allow one student from each school to go to Canberra, so representing Dukescliff Primary and Middle School will be ... Xander Beeston.'

Xander felt like the Bruise Brothers had punched him in the stomach.

'And that concludes this very special assembly,' said the principal. 'If Mr Steele and Xander could come to my office straight away, we can start making arrangements for the trip.'

As the principal left the stage, Xander stared straight ahead because he could not look his friends in the eye. By the time he turned to talk to them, they were gone, lost in a sea of swarming boys and girls.

Xander traipsed over to the principal's office and sat down in an uncomfortable old chair in the waiting room. He was soon joined by Mr Steele, who was in a foul mood.

'What are you up to?' he hissed.

'I don't know what's going on, sir …'

'Well I do, and you're going to tell Mr Whisker exactly how you cheated!'

'But Mr Steele …'

'I'm going to make sure the principal expels you over this, mark my …'

The door opened and a smiling Mr Whisker gestured for the two of them to enter his office. The principal plonked down behind his desk as Xander and Mr Steele sat in the two chairs opposite.

'Thanks for seeing us, Mr Whisker,' said Mr Steele. 'Xander has something to say to you, and I do as well.'

'No problems, Rupert — but firstly I want to say how proud I am … of *both* of you.'

'Both of us?' said Mr Steele.

'Rupert, to have the country's first and second ranked maths students in your class is a real feather in your cap. In fact, Tejas scored 100 per cent for the exam, and Xander only beat him because he was able to answer the bonus question that would have stumped most university professors.'

'Well, I'm not surprised *Tejas* did well, but I'm shocked that—'

'Don't be so modest, Rupert. There will be a nice little bonus coming your way because of these results.'

'Bonus?' said Mr Steele.

'Uh huh. *And* a salary increase.'

'A s-s-alary increase?'

'Oh yes. "Reward high performers" I always say,' said Mr Whisker. 'Now you mentioned you wanted to say something, Rupert?'

'Yes, um, I did … by the way, would this salary increase start straight away?'

'Of course.'

'Well in that case I just wanted to say … well done Xander!'

Xander's eyes nearly popped out of his head.

'Mr Whisker, there's something I need to tell you …' he started.

'No you don't,' urged Mr Steele. 'Your results speak for themselves.'

'Xander, you have put this school on the educational map,' said Mr Whisker. 'I can now attend any principals' conference with my head held high. Winning this competition means we'll be swamped with enrolments — off the record, we've been struggling to attract students lately. So your magnificent result has saved the school. I can't thank you enough — you're like a superhero. Anyway, I interrupted you — was there something you wanted to say?'

Xander looked at Mr Steele then back at the beaming principal.

'No, I guess not.' he said.

Xander finally caught up with Tee-Jay at lunchtime over by the basketball court. His friend was sitting down eating a salad roll next to Cat, who was peeling an orange.

'Hey,' said Xander.

'Hey … and congratulations,' said Tee-Jay

'Yeah, congratulations,' said Cat.

'It was a bit of shock,' mumbled Xander.

'I'll say!' agreed Tee-Jay.

Xander looked around sheepishly and said, 'Some days you're just in the zone, I suppose.'

'Xander, when have you *ever* been in the mathematics zone?' asked Cat.

Xander felt a wave of anger starting from behind his ear, which quickly spread throughout his body. He clenched his fists.

'Are you calling me stupid, Cat?'

'No, you're a very smart guy at most things … but not maths.'

'So you're calling me a cheat?'

Cat and Tee-Jay remained silent.

'Oh, so you're *both* calling me a cheat. What great friends you turned out to be!'

Xander stormed off and sat under the giant Monterey cypress tree that overlooked Cygnet Bay. The water was calm and still, in contrast to Xander, who was shaking with rage. He waited for Tee-Jay and Cat to come over to apologize. Then he waited some more. Eventually he peeked over his shoulder and discovered they were gone.

Xander exhaled as he pondered his situation. Phoebe had rushed off to boarding school, and now his two best friends had deserted him. For the first time in his life he felt … *lonely. I've only got one true friend*, he thought. *Shiver!*

He took out his sketch pad and special pen, and drew a scraggy-looking dog in a superhero costume standing on its hind legs. Behind him was a welcoming fireplace, an overflowing food bowl and an impressive four-poster bed. In the dog's speech bubble were the words, 'Home Sweet Home!'

He tapped the pen on his chin and whispered, 'See you after school, Shiver.'

As soon as the bell went, Xander rushed from class and was the first student out the school gate. He was so excited about seeing Shiver that he began to jog, but stopped when he saw flashing blue and red lights in the distance. *Shiver?*

Xander sprinted towards the footbridge. He could now make out an ambulance, two police cars and a crane that was lifting a delivery truck out of Cygnet Bay. A man on a trolley was being loaded into the ambulance. He wasn't moving and the two ambulance officers wore grim expressions on their faces.

Xander inspected the road. The dark squiggly tyre marks suggested that the truck had been totally out of control before plunging into the water. He turned to look at the truck and read the writing on its side: 'Mutley Dog Supplies: From food to bedding, we've got your pet covered!'

As the ambulance sped off, Xander pulled out his pen and stared at it in horror. But his feeling of guilt was quickly replaced by one of numbness, and he casually jogged past the police officers. As soon as he arrived at the footbridge, Shiver started barking.

'What's the matter, boy?'

Xander ducked under the bridge and his eyes widened.

Scattered on the ground were hundreds of cans of Mutley dog food, doggy bowls, toys and even a warm fluffy dog's bed.

'Talk about hitting the jackpot, Shiver!' said Xander.

He pulled the ring on a can of dog food and tipped the contents into a bowl. As he went to feed his canine friend, he spotted a dog's coat on the ground. It had the words 'Paw Relation' written on it.

'Classic! After you've eaten, we'll put that on you, boy.'

Xander placed the overflowing bowl in front of Shiver. The dog looked up at him, then moved his head from side to side.

'Don't act like that,' said Xander. 'Eat!'

Shiver sniffed the food, then started backing away.

'Not hungry, boy? That's cool. Let's put this cute little coat on to keep you warm, hey?'

The dog bared his teeth and started snarling.

'Shiver, stop it!' said Xander, confused.

But Shiver began barking and backed further away.

'So this is how it's going to be?' yelled Xander. 'You know what? You're a stupid dog and I wish I'd never helped you!'

Shiver stopped barking and stared at Xander with his big brown eyes.

Xander hurled the coat on the ground and stomped off.

Xander tossed and turned in bed.

Despite hearing on the evening news that the truck driver was going to be okay, he still felt responsible.

In a dream he saw Shiver wearing the 'Paw Relation' coat, which seemed to be getting tighter and tighter. The poor dog whimpered as he frantically tried to remove the coat with his teeth, and Xander woke up covered in sweat.

He sat up remembering his last words to Shiver and felt ill. After turning on his bedside light, he set his alarm for 6 a.m. *Pretty early for a Saturday*, he thought, before drifting off to sleep.

Xander was wide awake the instant his alarm went off. After a quick stretch he walked over and looked in the mirror.

'Something's different,' he whispered.

He stuck his tongue out at his reflection, then changed

into jeans and a plain white T-shirt. As he was tying the shoelaces of his red sneakers, he spotted the pen on the floor next to the bedside table. Instinctively he touched his right ear to confirm nothing was there. *Must have fallen out when I hopped into bed*, he thought.

Xander momentarily considered leaving the pen, but decided to pick it up and slip it into his pocket. After grabbing his backpack, he crept down the hallway towards the front door. Just as he was turning the door handle, a voice called out. 'Who are you, and what have you done with the *real* Xander?'

Xander spun around.

'Dad, what are you talking about?'

Mr Beeston, who was decked out in his fishing gear, dropped his rod then melodramatically placed his hands on his face.

'The *real* Xander never surfaces before eight o'clock on a Saturday, so you're clearly an imposter. Or … an *alien!*'

'Very funny,' said Xander. 'I just want to get a bit of exercise.'

'You are *definitely* an alien!' said Mr Beeston.

'So what do you think we'll be having for dinner?' asked Xander.

Mr Beeston picked up his rod.

'I was thinking … fish!'

'Was hoping you'd say that,' laughed Xander. 'See ya!'

He opened the door, walked out into Quarry Street and headed in the direction of the footbridge.

On the way he practised what he was going to say to Shiver: '"Hey boy, sorry about what I said" … No, too corny. How about, "I didn't mean it, Shiver"? … Nah, that's no good either!'

In the end he reasoned that dogs couldn't speak English, so a simple hug was the best way to go.

He arrived at the footbridge as the sun was rising over Cygnet Bay. A group of black swans descended gracefully before breaking the glass-like surface of the water.

'Shiver!' called out Xander.

After thirty seconds without a response, he walked under the bridge and waited for his eyes to adjust to the darkness. All the dog supplies were still there, but Shiver was nowhere to be seen. *Now I'm really alone*, he thought.

Suddenly he heard a skidding sound, accompanied by some boisterous voices nearby.

'Whoa! How cool are these bikes?' said Jeff Clagg.

'Yeah, these Laser Pro XJ5s are the best!' replied Tony.

Xander quietly edged further backwards into the darkness.

'What do ya wanna do now?' asked Jeff. 'How about we give the next loser we see an Egg Shampoo?'

Xander raised his eyebrows. *Egg Shampoo?*

'Nah, I'm keen to get home and play the new game Mum gave me.'

'Which one?'

'Mutant Space Zombies Death Zone 7.'

'That's supposed to have amazing graphics!'

'Let's go waste a few zombies, then we can get out the quad bikes later.'

'Cool!'

Xander put his hand into his pocket as the two bullies sped away. As soon as his fingers connected with the pen, he clenched his fist and frowned.

'Why should the Claggs have all the fun money can buy, while my family misses out?' he said.

He walked into the early morning sunlight, took a sketch pad from his backpack and sat down on the ground.

Eventually a smile appeared on his face and he started sketching a picture of a superhero called 'The Angler'. The Angler was a bald-headed, slightly overweight man who resembled his father. He was wielding a giant glowing fishing rod that had just hooked a fish with '$100,000' written on its side.

The Angler

He grinned as he reviewed his creation and, without thinking, slipped the pen back behind his ear.

That afternoon, Xander heard a commotion in the front yard and he and his mother rushed up the hallway to see what was going on. Xander stepped out the front door to see several news crews jostling for position as his father's rusty old station wagon approached along Quarry Street.

Mr Beeston parked the car and jumped out carrying his rod and a blue cooler box with a white lid. Instantly dozens of cameras starting clicking and journalists began shouting out questions. Xander listened in as a nearby reporter spoke directly to a camera.

'Local Dukescliff fisherman Cameron Beeston has just arrived home after the catch of a lifetime. While fishing off Vicar's Bluff, Mr Beeston managed to hook a giant Japanese sea bass — and not just any Japanese sea bass! This one had miraculously swum all the way from Japan carrying a special tag revealing that whoever caught the fish was the winner of a national Japanese fishing competition. And that winner receives 850,000,000 yen, which is approximately ten million dollars. That should keep Mr Beeston in fishing rods for a very long time!'

Xander looked at his mother and shook his head. *Don't do it Mum, please don't do it.*

Despite Xander's attempt at telepathic messaging, Mrs Beeston let out an incredibly high-pitched squeal, which caused the reporters to turn around.

'But you did it anyway,' muttered Xander.

'Let's find out what his wife thinks about becoming a muti-millionaire,' yelled out a journalist. This led to a stream of people with cameras and microphones rushing towards the front door.

Xander quickly slipped inside, leaving his mother to deal with the media scrum. He leant back against the door and smiled while gently rubbing the pen nestled safely behind his ear. As he started walking towards his bedroom, he heard his mum say, 'No, winning all this money won't change us a bit ...'

The next few days in the Beeston household were so frantic that Xander's parents took a week off work.

'It's not like we need the money anyway,' joked Mr Beeston.

There were TV and radio interviews from around the world, with everyone wanting to know how a fish released in Tokyo could have swum all the way to Dukescliff. Scientists were baffled, with several claiming it was impossible. But as Mr Beeston pointed out, 'If it was fake, they wouldn't have given me the money!'

The first thing Mrs Beeston did with the windfall was pay off all the outstanding medical bills relating to Phoebe's accident and rehabilitation.

'That is such a relief,' she said over breakfast. 'Do you think we should look at replacing the car next?'

'Probably,' said Mr Beeston. 'Nothing too flash, though.'

That night, when Xander came home from school, there was a red, two-door sports car in the drive.

'How's Dad going to go fishing in that?' he asked.

'That's my car, silly,' said Mrs Beeston. 'Your father bought himself a four-wheel drive.'

At dinner that night there wasn't much opportunity for chatting, as his parents were busy scrolling through websites on their new laptops, looking for products to buy.

'Since you guys bought yourselves cars, could I have a new bike?' asked Xander.

'Sure, mate, just write down the details and we'll get it delivered,' said Mr Beeston without looking up.

'And Mum, I really need a phone … for safety reasons.'

'No problem. In fact, we should all get new smartphones — I'll order them now!'

Xander smiled. *This is the life!*

The next night at dinner, Xander looked up from his phone to find his dad frowning while he was typing on his laptop.

'What's the matter?'

'Nothing … I went down to the beach in my new fishing gear this morning and the other fishermen laughed at me.'

'You looked great, Cam. Don't let that worry you,' said Mrs Beeston.

'So what are you going to do, Dad?'

'Might give the fishing away for a while. I mean, what's the point? We can eat steak every night if we want!'

'I'll tell you what we need, Cam,' said Mrs Beeston. 'A proper garage.'

'How come?'

'I've seen the way Mrs McNamara and Mr Lee have been staring at our new cars — I'm worried they might scratch them.'

'That's the problem with having nice things,' said Mr Beeston. 'I'll get someone onto it straight away.'

'What about Chris Christoforou?' suggested Mrs Beeston. 'He needs some work at the moment.'

'Nah, he charges too much. I think I'll shop around online.'

'Good call.'

Xander watched his parents typing away, and casually caressed the pen behind his ear. Suddenly he had an idea.

'Geez, those Clagg boys annoy me,' he said.

'What have they done now?' asked Mrs Beeston.

'I heard them boasting that they were the only family in Dukescliff that could afford quad bikes!'

'Really? Well let's show them!' said Mr Beeston.

Xander immediately pushed a button on his phone.

'I've just sent you a link, Dad — can you order a fluoro green one?'

Clickity-clack went the keyboard on Mr Beeston's laptop. 'Done!' he said smugly. 'Can you believe those Clagg boys?'

'No I can't,' said Mrs Beeston. 'But can you believe we've been married twenty years tomorrow?'

'Yes … yes I can,' said Mr Beeston in a slightly high-pitched voice.

He immediately started keying frantically on his laptop.

The following night, a magnificent anniversary dinner was home-delivered by Uber Eats.

'No one should have to cook on their anniversary,' said Mrs Beeston as she answered the door. A young woman handed over the bags and waited hopefully for a tip as the door was shut in her face.

After Xander helped dish up the food, the three of them sat down to celebrate the special twenty-year milestone. They all took a suspicious bite of the rockmelon bruschetta with citrus-flecked goat's cheese and prosciutto.

'What's this, Dad?' asked Xander.

'It's um … it's called … an entrée.'

There was a brief silence before Mrs Beeston said, 'So …'

'So … what?' asked Mr Beeston.

'Should we give each other our gifts now?'

'Yes of course!'

Mr Beeston dived under the table and pulled out a beautifully wrapped small square box.

'Ohhhhh!' said Mrs Beeston. 'You shouldn't have!'

She then reached under the table and pulled out a large envelope.

'Here you go, Cam — happy anniversary!'

Xander watched his parents enthusiastically rip open their presents.

'Oh … a *pendant*,' said Mrs Beeston. She held up a silver outline of a heart attached to a slender chain, and frowned.

'It's made of platinum — that's what you're supposed to buy for a twentieth anniversary … platinum,' explained Mr Beeston.

Mrs Beeston pulled out her laptop, as Mr Beeston examined the contents of the envelope.

'What is it?' asked Xander.

'A voucher for a room for two at the Sheraton Hotel in town … um, and a massage, facial and pedicure for two … two VIP passes for a shopping tour at some exclusive retail clothing stores … and two tickets to see the musical … *Cats*,' said Mr Beeston quietly.

Mrs Beeston looked up from her laptop and folded her arms.

'Nine hundred dollars.'

'What?'

'After twenty years of marriage, you spent a lousy nine hundred dollars on a stupid pendant! I spent more than twice that on *your* gift!'

'*My* gift? I'm pretty sure it's *your* gift. Why would I want a pedicure? Why would I want to go VIP shopping? And why buy me tickets to see *Cats* when you could have bought me tickets to see *Harry Potter*?'

Mrs Beeston sat back in her chair and glared at her husband.

'You said you didn't know who Harry Potter was,' she hissed.

'I might sleep on the couch tonight,' said Mr Beeston.

'No,' said Mrs Beeston, 'You'll *definitely* sleep on the couch tonight! And every other night, for all I care!'

Mrs Beeston stomped off to the bedroom and slammed the door. Mr Beeston shrugged his shoulders.

'Now we've got Netflix, I'd rather sleep on the couch anyway,' he said.

CHAPTER

12

Mr and Mrs Beeston refused to talk to each other after their disastrous present swap. This made dinner time especially awkward.

'Xander, can you ask your father to pass the salt?'

'Dad, can you pass Mum the salt?'

'Sure. And can you ask your mother for the pepper?'

'Mum, can you pass Dad the pepper?'

'Of course, honey.'

Xander watched his parents eating their home-delivered food in silence. As he brushed back his hair, his fingers touched the pen, and another idea popped into his head. He smiled and waited patiently for his mum to finish her meal.

'Good night, Xander,' said Mrs Beeston.

She picked up her son's plate while ignoring her husband's, and headed to the kitchen before stomping off to the bedroom.

After he heard the door slam, Xander turned to his father.

'Hey Dad, it's Tee-Jay's birthday on Saturday and I need to get him a present.'

'Did you have any ideas?'

'Well, because he missed out on the trip to Canberra, I want to get him something good.'

'How good?'

'I was thinking a quad bike …'

'A quad bike? Do you have any idea how much they cost?' Xander shook his head.

'That's exactly what Mum said. She said she wouldn't waste her money buying something like that.'

'*Her* money? She said *her* money? Who caught that fish?'

'You did, Dad.'

'That's right. So it's *my* money, and if *I* say you can give Tee-Jay a quad bike, then you can. In fact, I'll order it right now.'

'Thanks Dad! You're the best. Oh, can you get him a fluoro orange one — I'll send you the link …'

Xander arrived at Tee-Jay's house wearing a designer T-shirt, designer jeans and a brand new pair of Triple Pump XYZ Warrior sneakers.

Mrs Sah answered the door and raised her eyebrows as she looked him up and down.

'Hi Xander. Glad you could make it — Tee-Jay wasn't sure you were coming.'

'Yeah, we haven't been talking much lately,' mumbled Xander.

He walked inside and followed the sounds of the party to the lounge room. Cat was playing DJ and another ten kids from school were dancing or standing around sipping soft drinks.

'Hi, Beast,' said Timmy Fontaine.

'Not now, mate. I need to speak to Tee-Jay.'

Xander brushed past Timmy and walked towards the birthday boy, who was topping up a few drinks.

When Tee-Jay saw him he narrowed his eyes.

'Hey,' he said.

'Hey,' replied Xander.

The awkward silence that followed was magnified because a song had just finished playing.

'Um, can I get you a drink?' asked Tee-Jay.

'Thanks … but first I want to give you my gift.'

'Sure.'

'It's outside.'

'Huh?'

'I'll show you.'

Xander started walking towards the door, and Tee-Jay followed.

'You usually give me a really awesome drawing, so how come we have to go outside?'

'You'll see!'

They walked outside and Xander motioned to the street.

'Ta dah!'

'What?'

'The quad bike.'

'What about it?'

'It's your present. Now we'll be able to ride together on weekends …'

'What's going on?' asked Mrs Sah from the doorway.

'Um, Xander gave me … a quad bike,' said Tee-Jay.

Mrs Sah's jaw dropped.

'Uh, Tejas can't possibly accept such an expensive gift, Xander. I'm sorry.'

Xander felt a power surge from behind his ear and he clenched his fists. He turned to Tee-Jay and said, 'Do you want the bike or not?'

Tee-Jay took a deep breath.

'No … but thanks anyway.'

Xander watched his friend walk back inside.

'You coming in?' asked Mrs Sah.

'No, I'm good,' said Xander.

As soon as the front door shut, Xander took out his phone and rang his father.

'Dad, you won't believe this! Mrs Sah said Tee-Jay couldn't accept the bike because it cost too much.'

'Gee, you try to be nice and … don't worry mate, they're just jealous of our success.'

'Thanks, Dad — I'll be home soon.'

Xander hung up and walked over to the shiny new quad bike.

'Hey, Beast, is that your bike?'

He spun around to see Tony Clagg standing next to his brother Jeff.

'Yeah,' said Xander as casually as he could. 'I got this one, *and* a green one.'

Tony pointed at Xander's feet.

'Are they the new Triple Pump XYZ Warriors?'

'Yep.'

'Nice,' said Jeff.

'We're taking our bikes out for a burn tomorrow — wanna come?' asked Tony.

Xander folded his arms and nodded. 'Why not?' he said.

'Okay, meet us around ten o'clock near Vicar's Bluff.

There's heaps of cool jumps inside the old shell grit quarry.'

Xander's eyes widened. 'Jumps?'

'Yeah ... unless you're too chicken?' asked Jeff.

'Chicken? I love jumps. Just hope they're big enough.'

Xander had never been over a jump in his life and didn't want to look foolish in front of the Bruise Brothers. After arriving home, he lay on his bed to consider his options. *I could go to the quarry and practice, or ...*

Xander jumped up, grabbed the pen from behind his ear and started a drawing with the caption, 'The Beast of Bumps!' It featured a kid with a mop of hair like his own doing a somersault over a massive jump on a motorcycle.

As Xander reviewed his sketch he smiled. *All set for tomorrow.*

The next morning, Xander spotted Tony and Jeff in the distance. He put his quad bike into first gear, gave it a few revs and then popped the clutch. The front of the bike shot up into the air and he cruised over to the Clagg boys on two wheels.

'Nice,' said Tony.

'Whatevs,' said Xander.

The trio zipped off in single file, with Tony in the lead. As soon as they entered the deserted quarry, Xander could see several small hills … and also an enormous one.

'I'll go first,' announced Tony. He went over the three small mounds, soaring way off the ground at the top of each one.

'Good air!' yelled out Jeff.

'Yeah, really excellent with the, um, air,' said Xander.

Then it was Jeff's turn. 'Watch and learn,' he said cockily. He clicked his bike into gear and went over the bumps almost as expertly as his older brother.

After the Clagg boys rejoined him, Xander gave his bike a few revs.

'Let's see what you got,' challenged Tony.

'Watch and learn,' said Xander. He took off like a bull out of a gate, his tyres sending stones and a huge cloud of dust into the air.

Xander sped past the three smaller hills, directly towards the giant one. He raced up the steep incline, and as soon as he reached the top he leant back on the bike and performed a perfect mid-air somersault. He even took his hands off the handlebars and put them behind his head as if he was taking a snooze. As he was spinning around he could see the blue of the cloudless sky, then the green of the ocean that bordered the quarry at the base of a cliff.

He landed perfectly on the downward slope and flew back to join the Clagg boys. He pulled up with a spectacular sliding stop, and Tony and Jeff stared at him with their mouths wide open.

As the dust settled Tony said, 'That was … awesome!'

'Yeah, that was full on!' agreed Jeff.

Xander looked at the two brothers and said, 'Are you guys going to have a go … or is the big hill too scary?'

Jeff went bright red and said, 'I'll have a go.'

'Don't be stupid,' said Tony, who revved up his bike set off to tackle the smaller hills again.

Xander shook his head and muttered under his breath, 'So lame.'

'What was that?' asked Jeff.

'Nothing.'

'You don't think I can do the big jump, do you, Beast?'

'It doesn't matter, because your brother told you not to …'

'Tony's not the boss of me!'

'Well, it kinda sounds like he is …'

'I'll show you,' said Jeff revving up his bike.

He shot off with a determined look on his face just as Tony was coming back.

'Don't be an idiot,' he yelled after his brother.

Xander shook his head like a wise old grandpa. 'I tried to talk him out of it, Tone,' he said.

He watched as Jeff went scorching past the smaller jumps and headed straight for the big one. The bike raced up the hill but hit the top on an angle, and when Jeff leant back, the bike sailed way off to the right. Instead of landing on the downward slope of the hill, Jeff disappeared over the other side. The side with a sheer cliff overlooking the rocky coast-line.

Tony swore loudly then took off looking for his brother, with Xander close behind.

When they arrived at the cliff, Xander nervously peered over it. *OMG!* Motorbike parts were scattered over the rocks below. Xander looked across at Tony, who had tears in his eyes. Suddenly he heard a voice that seemed to come from above them.

'Little help?'

He looked up to see Jeff clinging to a lone pine tree next to the cliff's edge. There were scratches all over his face and his jacket was caught on one of the branches.

Tony quickly scaled the tree and freed his brother's top so he could get down.

'You okay, Jeff?' asked Xander.

'I th-think s-so.'

'What about your bike?'

'We'll just tell Dad it was stolen,' said Tony. 'Come on, let's get out of here.'

Xander watched Jeff hop onto the back of his brother's bike as if nothing had happened.

'So, where to now?' he asked.

Tony delved into a compartment near the handlebars and retrieved two eggs. He tossed one to Xander and handed the other one to Jeff.

'Time for an Egg Shampoo!'

As Tony shot off, Xander momentarily hesitated before starting up his bike and following after him.

They exited the quarry and headed back towards Vicar's Bluff. Up ahead Xander could see a boy carrying a fishing rod and a small basket. It was Timmy Fontaine.

As the Bruise Brothers went by Timmy, Jeff hurled his egg, hitting the defenceless young fisherman on the shoulder.

Timmy spun around to see where the oval missile had come from, just as the second quad bike was roaring by. Xander threw his egg.

Splat!

Timmy's head was instantly covered in a yellow, gooey mess. Jeff laughed and yelled out, 'Direct hit!'

Xander stared straight into Timmy's eyes. Eyes filled with

a mixture of confusion and hurt.

He quickly looked away then sped off to catch up to his new friends.

CHAPTER
13

The Beeston's dinner table was covered with Uber Eats bags, because Xander and his parents now ordered their meals separately to avoid having to share.

Xander slapped his father's hand as he reached out for one of the bags in front of him.

'Don't even think about it! That's *my* sweet and sour pork.'

'But that's what I ordered …'

'Find your own bag!'

Xander went back to checking online reviews of the latest Xbox games, when he suddenly remembered something important.

'Hey, when does Phoebe get back?'

'Who?' said Mr Beeston without looking up from his laptop.

'Phoebe … your daughter!'

'Um … ask your mother.'

'Mum?'

'Not sure, honey — it's in my diary by the phone. Can't check right now — busy on eBay.'

Xander rolled his eyes and walked over to the diary.

'It's five p.m. … tomorrow!'

Mr and Mrs Beeston looked up as if they had been zapped with an electric shock.

'Tomorrow? Well, someone has to pick her up from the train station,' said Mrs Beeston. 'I can't — I've got Pilates.'

'Me either,' declared Mr Beeston. 'I'm booked in for a pedicure.'

Mrs Beeston's eyes narrowed as she stared at her husband.

'I know!' he said. 'Let's hire a limo to pick her up, she'll love that!'

Mrs Beeston pushed out her bottom lip and nodded.

'That's the smartest thing you've said since … ever.'

Xander broke into a grin as he opened the front door.

'Hey sis!'

'Hey bro!'

Phoebe dropped her bags and gave him a hug.

'What was with the limo pick-up?' she asked.

'Well, Mum's at Pilates and Dad's getting a pedicure.'

'Say what?'

Xander rolled his eyes and said, 'Come on in.'

He picked up one of the bags and Phoebe followed him down the hallway. As they walked past the lounge room, she stopped and stared.

'OMG! That's the *biggest* TV I've ever seen!'

'It's *so* good for Xbox,' said Xander.

'Xbox? And that's a new couch — that's huge too!'

'It needs to be big — Dad sleeps there now.'

'Huh?'

Phoebe put down her bag and walked over to the far corner of the room. She picked up the metal detector and frowned.

'What's with The Seeker? There's cobwebs all over it,' she said.

'That's terrible!' said Xander. 'Julie is going to be in so much trouble!'

'Who's Julie?'

'The cleaner.'

'The what?'

Their brother–sister conversation was interrupted when Mrs Beeston burst in. Xander barely had time to cover his ears before she let out a giant high-pitched squeal.

'Eeeeeeee! Come and give me a hug!'

Phoebe rushed over and embraced her mother. They each took a step back and looked at each other.

'Mum … is that … *active*wear?'

'Yes, it's the Alo Yoga range — Taylor Swift wears it.'

'What's wrong with a good old pair of tracksuit pants?'

'I couldn't possibly be seen in the main street wearing tracksuit pants!'

'Mum, you *always* used to be seen in the main street wearing them!'

'I don't think so, honey …'

The sound of the front door opening brought a scowl to Mrs Beeston's face. 'Sounds like your father's home.'

Mr Beeston walked into the lounge room flashing a warm smile.

He was wearing a grey sleeveless T-shirt with 'NVR STP' on the front. It was fairly tight, emphasizing his middle-aged spread and his skinny arms, which had clearly never been in the same room as a set of weights.

'Hi, Phoebs,' said Mr Beeston. 'Love your Riverview uniform.'

'Thanks Dad, and your top is, um …'

'Missing a few vowels!' said Xander.

'Hey, David Beckham wears this top,' said Mr Beeston.

'And I'm sure people get you two confused all the time!'

said Xander.

'Oh leave him alone,' said Phoebe. 'Dad, one of the things I really missed was having your fresh fish for dinner.'

'Well, we're having a special dinner tonight, but it's not fish,' said Mrs Beeston. 'We're eating Spanish!'

'When did you learn to cook Spanish?' asked Phoebe. But her question was answered by the sound of doorbell.

'Uber Eats is here!' said Xander. 'You're going to love the paella, sis.'

Phoebe screwed up her face.

'The pay what now?'

'Go and freshen up, Phoebs — can't wait to hear all your news.' said Mrs Beeston.

Fifteen minutes later, when they were all seated around the table, Mr Beeston tapped his glass.

'Welcome home, Phoebs. We've really missed you,' he said.

'And *I* missed you so much *I* bought you a present,' said Mrs Beeston, eying her husband. She pulled out an expensive-looking phone and handed it to Phoebe.

'Wow, um, thanks.'

Xander gave his sister a thumbs-up then started playing on his own phone. He noticed his mother was already playing Candy Crush, and his father was laughing at a funny YouTube clip.

'School's really good,' said Phoebe.

Xander looked up in shock. Nowadays it was rare for someone to start a conversation over dinner.

'That's fantastic, honey,' said Mrs Beeston.

'Great news,' said Mr Beeston.

Neither of them looked up from their phones.

'The teachers are really good and the athletics track is amazing.'

'That's fantastic, honey,' said Mrs Beeston.

'Great news,' said Mr Beeston.

'And if we get caught talking after lights out, we get locked in a dungeon and they make us eat rats.'

'That's fantastic, honey,' said Mrs Beeston.

'Great news,' said Mr Beeston.

Phoebe looked at Xander and shook her head.

'I'm not feeling hungry so I might go and unpack,' she said.

'That's fantastic, honey,' said Mrs Beeston

'Great news,' said Mr Beeston.

After Xander finished eating, he put a few of the Uber Eats bags into the bin and headed to his room. It was still early in the evening, and the last of the sun's rays were streaming through the window. He sat down at his desk and pushed back his hair. As soon as his fingers touched the pen, he was overcome by an unpleasant wave of energy. He scowled and folded his arms just as there was a gentle knock on the door. He turned as Phoebe entered and sat on his bed.

After an awkward silence, he said, 'Well?'

'What's going on?'

'What do you mean?'

'No one talks at dinner, Dad's sleeping on the couch and Mum's wearing *active wear*!'

'So?'

'You've all changed!'

'I haven't,' snapped Xander.

'Really? How's Shiver going?'

'Well … he sort of … ran away.'

Phoebe shook her head.

'Have you found out how the Cruzes' alpacas died?'

'Um, no … I'm not really speaking to Cat and Tee-Jay at the moment.'

'No way! So who are you hanging out with?'

'Um, I suppose … Tony and Jeff Clagg …'

'The Bruise Brothers? You have got to be kidding me!'

'They're actually not that bad once you get to know them. They know all the cool spots for quad bikes, and Mr Clagg's got this amazing speed boat called "Jealous Much?" …'

Phoebe's face went bright red.

'The Claggs! OMG Xander!'

'Don't get angry with me! If anything you should be thanking me!'

'How come?'

'Because if it wasn't for me you'd still be in a wheelchair!'

Phoebe looked into Xander's eyes.

'Why would you say that?'

'Because it's true. Thanks to this!' Xander took the pen from behind his ear and waved it above his head.

'It's a pen,' said Phoebe.

'And whatever I draw with it … happens.'

'Quit fooling around Xander …'

'You don't believe me? Well take a look at this!' Xander opened a drawer and pulled out a pile of ink sketches.

'Remember when you saved that baby?'

Phoebe nodded.

'Well, here's the drawing I did the night before. And here's the one I did just before you were healed. This one I did when Dad took on Mr Clagg, here's me beating up the Bruise brothers, and here's Dad catching the fish that made us rich.'

'H-how do I know you didn't draw them *after* all those things happened …'

'Phoebs, what am I like at maths?'

'Not good.'

Xander handed his sister the 'Calculator Boy' drawing.

'After I drew that, I topped the country in a maths test.'

Phoebe examined the drawing and shook her head.

'So, you cheated in that maths competition? The one your best friend was desperate to win? You really have become a beast!'

Xander gripped the pen tightly.

'This is the thanks I get? You can walk because of *me*. You got your scholarship back because of *me*. Our family doesn't have to worry about money because of *me*. Yet somehow, *I'm* the bad guy? You are so ungrateful, I can't even look at you.'

Xander stormed out of his bedroom then down the hallway, before stomping out the front door. 'Unbelievable,' he muttered.

Mrs McNamara and Mr Lee were chatting on the footpath, but stopped when they saw Xander.

'Are your parents organizing the street party again this year?' asked Mr Lee.

'Who cares?' said Xander without slowing down.

There was a brilliant orange sunset over Cygnet Bay, but it hardly registered with Xander.

'No one appreciates me,' he mumbled. He kept walking without a destination in mind, and eventually arrived at the footbridge. With a shrug of his shoulders he ambled underneath and lay down on the comfortable dog's bed. He took the pen from behind his ear, placed it on the ground next to him and shut his eyes.

His anger began to subside, and he remembered the troubled expression on his sister's face when he had stormed out. He also remembered how Timmy Fontaine had looked at him after receiving the Egg Shampoo. *I pushed Tee-Jay and Cat away*, he recalled, *then Shiver … and now Phoebs … maybe I am a beast?*

Xander picked up the pen and went to put it behind his ear, but stopped. He slipped it into his pocket instead and started jogging back towards Quarry Street.

It was dark when he arrived home, so he was surprised to discover that all the lights were turned off. He opened the door and flicked on the hallway light.

'Anyone home?'

Xander spotted a note on the floor and recognized his mother's handwriting.

> *Xander, poor Phoebs had a relapse, we've had to rush*
> *her to hospital. Call me and we'll organize a taxi so*
> *you can meet us there.*
> *Love Mum. xx*

Xander sprinted to his room and stared at the bed.

His drawing of Phoebe being cured, as well as the one of Mr Beeston catching the fish lay on his pillow. They had been ripped into tiny pieces.

'Phoebs, what have you done?'

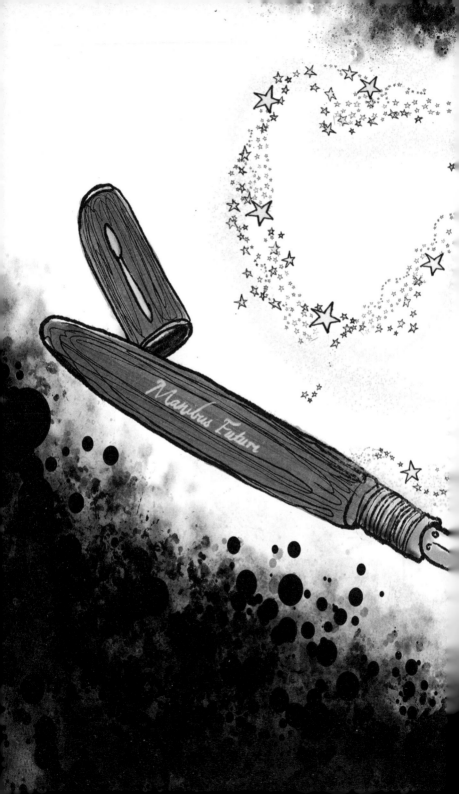

CHAPTER

14

The Beeshort Hospital was a thirty-minute taxi ride from Dukescliff. But for Xander, it seemed a lot longer. He sat in the back chewing his fingernails as the talkative old driver shared his views on education.

'Back in my day, we learnt the three Rs: reading, writing and arithmetic ...'

Xander raised his eyebrows. *The three Rs? Maybe they should have focused on the one S — spelling!*

'Nowadays, you kids learn about hip hop music and graffiti art, but that won't get you a job ...'

Xander shook his head and stared out the window. A storm was approaching and he spotted a small herd of black and white cows huddled together in a paddock. He immediately thought about the Cruzes' alpacas and wondered if any more had died.

His thoughts were distracted as the car made a sharp

right turn.

'… and that's why teachers should be allowed to use the cane on their students,' said the driver as the taxi stopped in front of the hospital. It was an old, faded brick building, which included several new sections that had been added in a random manner. No attempt had been made to match the architecture, which was why the locals referred to it as 'Frankenstein's Monster'.

Xander leapt out of the cab as a spectacular bolt of lightning flashed in the sky. Rain was pelting down and even though it was only a short distance to the hospital doors, his clothes were drenched by the time he made it inside. He raced over to the reception desk where a well-dressed young man wearing a phone headset was sitting.

'Excuse me, can you please tell me which room Phoebe Beeston is in?'

The man held up his finger to indicate he was on an important call.

'Uh huh … uh huh … okay then … I'll bring dessert … no you hang up … no you first … no you hang up …'

The man looked up at Xander.

'Unbelievable … she hung up!'

'Um, that's too bad. As I said, can you please tell me where Phoebe Beeston's room is?'

The young man looked at Xander's dripping wet clothes and rolled his eyes.

'Now listen carefully, because I'm only going to say this once. You need to follow the blue line painted on the floor through the cafeteria, and past the florist until you come to a set of lifts. Take a lift to the third floor and follow the yellow line across the walkway past X-rays until you reach another set of lifts. If you reach the maternity ward, that means you've gone too far and you'll need to turn around. Anyway, you take the lift to the sixth floor and follow a green line until you hit a double door. You then turn right down a long corridor and that gets you to the patients' rooms, and your sister is in room six-eighteen.'

'Six-eighteen,' repeated Xander. 'Got it — thanks.'

The man gave a fleeting sarcastic smile, and Xander turned around.

Bang! He accidentally collided with a nurse.

'Are you okay?' she asked.

'I'm a bit lost, actually. Can you tell me how to get to room six-eighteen?'

'Sure, I'm heading that way myself — follow me.'

Xander gave the annoying receptionist a friendly wave, then set off after the young woman in the light blue scrubs.

He thanked the nurse once they arrived at Phoebe's room,

then hesitated before entering. Through the door he could see his parents seated at the end of the bed. *OMG*, he thought, *they're holding hands!*

'Glad you could get here so quickly, Xander,' said Mr Beeston. 'Come and talk to Phoebs while your mum and I chat to the doctor.'

Mrs Beeston gave Xander a warm hug before trailing her husband out of the room.

Suddenly he was alone with his sister, who was connected to an IV drip and wearing a blue patient's gown.

'Hey, bro,' she said softly.

Xander scanned across to the wheelchair next to the bed. 'Phoebs ... why?'

'That pen ... or whatever it is ... it's not good for you.'

'I was trying to help ...'

'And look what happened. Our family's a mess and you're BFFs with the Claggs!' Xander went bright red and looked down at the floor.

'Promise me you won't do any more drawings with that pen,' said Phoebe.

Xander took a deep breath. 'Phoebs, I promise I'll try ...'

The intense conversation was interrupted by the return of their parents.

'We have to give your sister some rest,' said Mrs Beeston.

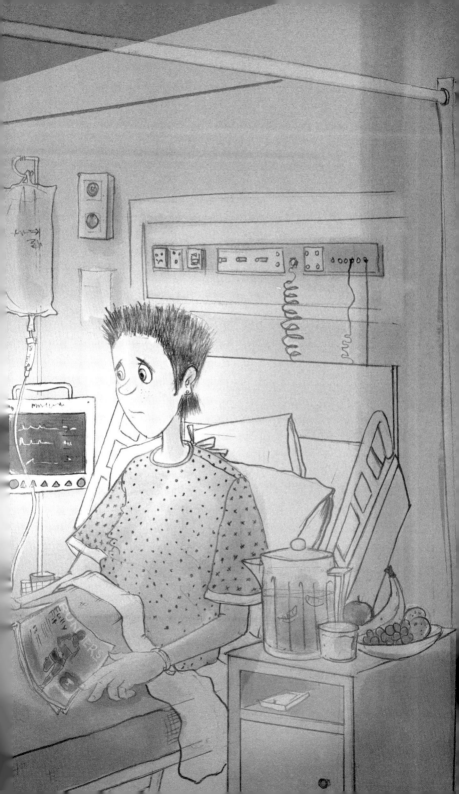

'But we'll be back to see you tomorrow, Phoebs,' said Mr Beeston.

Xander did his best to muster a smile and nodded at his sister.

At 1 a.m. Xander was woken by the sound of the telephone. He remembered Grandpa Beeston had once told him, 'No one ever calls with good news after midnight'.

He flicked on his bedside light and glanced at the pen sitting on his desk. After resisting the urge to pick it up, he slipped out into the corridor to listen to his father on the phone.

'… no, I don't speak Japanese … English … Anglaise? … Money? … What? … but we've already spent … that's not fair … no, I didn't read the rules … surely there's some way to compromise … well you don't sound very sorry … you have a nice night too!'

Xander heard the phone slam down and then his mother's voice.

'What is it, Cam?'

'The money for that fish I caught … we have to give it back.'

'B-b-but why?'

'They said there was a mistake, and according to the rules you had to be a Japanese citizen to win.'

'Cam, what about Phoebe's hospital bills? And your court case with Tristan — without a decent lawyer, you might end up in jail ...'

Xander crept back to his room and hopped into bed. As he lay on his back staring at the ceiling, a golden flash of light caught the corner of his eye. It had come from the pen on his desk, and instinctively he reached out for it. But an image of Phoebe in hospital popped into his mind, and he quickly withdrew his hand and rolled over. Eventually he drifted off into a fitful sleep.

The next morning Xander woke up and crawled out of bed. He felt ill and his hands were shaking.

He managed to avoid the magnetic pull of the pen on his desk and went to the kitchen where his mum was sitting at the table. Her eyes were puffy and she was half-heartedly eating some toast with apricot jam.

'You okay?' asked Xander.

'Not really,' admitted Mrs Beeston. 'How about you?'

'Been better.'

'Well we're allowed to visit Phoebe this afternoon, so that's something …'

Mrs Beeston started sobbing and Xander put his arm around her.

'Sorry, Xander … I'm just worried about Phoebs … and your father … and all of us.'

'I know.' Xander looked over to the corner of the lounge room, and his eyes landed on The Seeker.

'Hey Mum, I need to do something,' he said.

He walked to his bedroom and studied the pen on his desk from the doorway. He shook his head and started back to the kitchen, before turning around once more. This time he went to his desk and pulled a piece of paper from the drawer.

'It's just *one* more,' he mumbled.

Xander picked up the pen. Immediately he felt much better, and as he started to draw his hands stopped shaking.

His picture was of a smiling young superhero with a mass of curly hair holding a lethal-looking metal detector. In the foreground was a treasure chest overflowing with jewels, and on the inside lid was the word 'Finito'. At the top he added the words, 'Finders, Keepers'.

Xander put the sketch in a drawer, grabbed his backpack and headed to the lounge room. He picked up The Seeker, brushed off the cobwebs and quietly slipped out the front door.

Finders, Keepers

When he reached the Black Lighthouse he sat down to catch his breath. He had never used The Seeker before but it seemed pretty simple to operate. He flicked the switch to 'on' and the machine immediately beeped once, then went silent. There was an empty Coke can on the ground next to him and Xander ran the circular head of The Seeker over it. A high-pitched sound leapt from the detector and Xander quickly moved it away from the can. *And I thought Mum and Phoebe's squeals were bad!* he thought.

He jumped to his feet, picked up the can and popped it into a bin before heading towards some nearby bushes. He was soon surrounded by dense tea trees and boobialla, and he stopped to get his bearings.

If I was Finito, he wondered, *where would I hide my treasure?*

To his left the sun had managed to break through the thick canopy of trees, creating a spotlight effect on a distant pile of rocks. *Aha!*

Xander headed in that direction through the thick bushes, and soon his arms were scratched and bleeding. Once he reached his destination, he took a few deep breaths and studied the mini mountain of rocks stacked in front of him. They were well worn and infused with weeds, suggesting they had been there a long time. He waved The Seeker over the pile and instantly a high beeping noise rang out.

'Shhh! Don't tell everyone!' he said to the metal detector. He started removing the large basalt stones, and just over an hour later, the job was completed.

Xander picked up The Seeker and waved it over the bare patch of dirt. This time the squeal was even higher and louder.

He started clawing at the light brown, sandy soil, and soon hit a solid object. After some more concentrated digging, the top of a small metal rectangular box was revealed. The soil was quite loose, and despite a few damaged fingernails he was able to unearth the chest, which was about the size of a loaf of bread.

Xander lifted the lid and his eyes widened — it was jam-packed with colourful jewels.

As the sun hit the diamonds, rubies and emeralds, they sparkled brilliantly. He smiled, slammed the lid shut and shoved the treasure into his backpack.

When the Beestons arrived at Beeshort Hospital that afternoon, they bumped into Phoebe's doctor on the ground floor.

'Xander, you go and see Phoebs while we chat to Dr Collins,' said Mrs Beeston.

'I can wait,' said Xander.

'Don't be silly — we might be a while,' said Mr Beeston.

Xander nodded and slowly headed to his sister's room. He started to perspire and his stomach felt as if it was tied in knots. He walked through the door and over to Phoebe's bed. To his relief she was asleep, but as soon as he sat down her eyes opened and she stared at him.

'I'm sorry, Phoebs.'

Tears welled in his sister's eyes.

'You used the pen again, didn't you?'

Xander nodded, unable to meet her gaze.

'You promised me!'

'I know … but you don't understand how hard it is …'

Phoebe shook her head and waited for Xander to look her in the eye. 'Is it harder than being told you'll never walk again?'

CHAPTER
15

Xander stared at the pen on his desk, fighting the urge to pick it up.

Its power had never been this strong, and his arm involuntarily reached out for it. As his hand moved closer, he thought of Phoebe's words. *Harder than being told you'll never walk again?*

As he was about to touch the pen, his hand veered to the right and picked up a ruler instead. Xander then pushed the pen into the top drawer and slammed it shut. He was sweating and his hands were trembling, but a satisfied smile appeared on his face.

After taking a deep breath, he left his bedroom, went into the lounge room and picked up the copy of the *Dukescliff Daily* sitting on the coffee table. The front-page headline read, 'Bungalow by the Beach Set to Close!' Xander quickly scanned the first paragraph.

Due to a lack of funding, children's charity The Bungalow by the Beach is closing next month. It is a sad day for Dukescliff because this amazing charity has provided children with holidays and leadership programs for over one hundred years.

Xander sighed. Reading about a charity that had selflessly helped so many children — including children like Phoebe — made him think about his behaviour since he first bought the pen. It wasn't good, and it certainly wasn't selfless. His face went bright red as overwhelming feelings of shame and remorse coursed through his body.

With Phoebe's words running through his mind, Xander knew what he had to do. He put down the newspaper then tiptoed down the hallway towards the front door.

As he picked up his backpack as quietly as he could, he heard his father on the phone.

'…but I can't afford a lawyer … yes I know the charges are serious … no, I don't want to end up in jail …'

Xander stopped and looked back towards his bedroom. He could feel the pull of the pen but he shook his head and headed out the door.

The Bungalow by the Beach was a sprawling, old two-storey house located at the end of Dukescliff's most expensive street, The Boulevard. Its exterior desperately needed a coat of paint, the garden was overgrown, and some of the guttering had come away from the roof.

Xander made sure no one was around before sneaking up the well-worn brick steps to the front door. He took the box of jewels from his backpack and stuck a yellow sticky note on top with the words 'Finders, Keepers'.

After putting the chest down, he pressed the doorbell and bolted to the bushes on the other side of the road. A tall man in a dark suit opened the door and Xander immediately ducked down. He kept watching as the man picked up the metal box and looked inside. A beaming smile appeared on the man's face, and then he did something unexpected. He stared directly at Xander and nodded his head, before heading back inside. The twinkle in the man's eyes seemed familiar, and suddenly Xander remembered where he'd seen it before.

The man who sold me the pen!

He shook his head and smiled. *Nah — just my imagination.*

Before school the next day, Xander spotted Tee-Jay and Cat standing under the Monterey cypress tree. He tried to channel his sister's courage as he marched over.

'Cat, Tee-Jay ... sorry for being a complete jerk,' he said. 'I don't expect you to forgive me, but I want you to know I'm really sorry.'

Cat and Tee-Jay exchanged a quick glance.

'Um, Xander ...' started Cat.

Xander held up his hand. 'Please let me finish apologizing, then I'll go, I promise.'

Cat and Tee-Jay nodded.

'Tee-Jay, apart from being a total jerk, I want to say sorry for cheating on that maths exam. It was a really low act, and I don't deserve your friendship.'

Tee-Jay folded his arms and stared at Xander. 'So you *did* cheat?'

Xander nodded then looked at Cat. 'Cat, apart from being a total jerk, I want to apologize for not helping with your alpacas. I found a suspicious trapdoor at Clagg's Cannery, but thanks to me they doubled the security, making it almost impossible to go back.'

It was Cat's turn to fold her arms. 'How long ago did you find the trapdoor?'

'Six weeks ...'

'You've waited *six weeks* to tell me!' said Cat shaking her head.

There was an awkward silence as Xander reached into his backpack and pulled out a drawing. It was a pencil sketch of Xander's head on a donkey's body standing next to Cat and Tee-Jay who were dressed as superheroes. At the bottom it said, 'Please forgive me for being a complete *ass!*'

He handed it to Cat and said, 'Sorry to both of you — I'm going to try as hard as I can to fix things.'

Cat inspected the drawing, and Xander thought he saw the briefest of smiles before she handed it to Tee-Jay.

'Thanks for hearing me out,' he said.

Xander walked off and headed towards Jeff and Tony Clagg. They were on the edge of the oval, doing what they did best — being bullies. Jeff was holding down Timmy Fontaine while Tony administered what the Bruise Brothers called 'The Two-Finger Typewriter'. This merely consisted of Tony poking a helpless kid in the chest with two fingers. It was a very simple, yet painful bullying technique.

'Stop!' yelled Xander.

Jeff and Tony looked at him quizzically.

'Do you want us to stop so you can give him another Egg Shampoo?' asked Jeff.

'No, I want you stop because Timmy's my mate.'

Tony slowly stood up. 'Have we got a problem?'

'Yes we do. I'm sick of you pushing everyone around.'

'So am I!' came a voice from behind Xander. *Tee-Jay?*

He spun around to see Tee-Jay and Cat standing in front of another thirty kids.

'And me,' said Cat.

'Me too,' said another student, and then the rest all yelled out, 'Me too!'

Tony took a step back as Jeff let go of Timmy and jumped to his feet.

'You're now back on our list, Beast!' said Tony. The Bruise Brothers jogged off and Xander helped Timmy to his feet.

'Sorry about the egg,' he said.

'That's cool,' said Timmy.

'No, it wasn't,' said Xander.

He looked at Tee-Jay and Cat and the students behind them and nodded. 'Thanks.'

'Where are you off to now?' asked Cat.

'The principal's office.'

'Do you have an appointment?' asked a frowning Miss Hopkins.

'No,' said Xander. 'But I need to see Mr Whisker straight

away …'

'Bad luck — if you don't have an appointment, you don't get to see him,' replied Miss Hopkins.

Right at that moment, Mr Whisker walked out of his office and spotted Xander.

'Here he is, the number one student in the country! Come on in, my door is always open.'

Xander glanced at Miss Hopkins, who looked as if she had bitten into a lemon. He shrugged his shoulders then followed Mr Whisker into his office.

'So what can I do for you?' asked the principal.

Xander took a deep breath and once again replayed his sister's words in his head. *Harder than being told you'll never walk again?*

'I have to confess about doing something … really bad.'

'Really bad?'

Xander nodded. 'In that national maths test, I kind of a cheated a bit. Well a lot actually.'

Mr Whisker's jaw dropped. 'You what?'

'Cheated — as in I had all the answers before the test … I'm really sorry. I'm actually pretty bad at maths …'

'B-b-but you're supposed to be going to Canberra in two weeks! I'm going to be a laughing stock at the next headmaster's conference!'

'What about Tee-Jay?'

'Who?'

'Tejas Sah. He scored the best "non-cheating" result in the country so you still have the number one student. He can represent the school in Canberra.'

'Mmm, that's true,' said Mr Whisker, pushing a button on his phone. 'Miss Hopkins, can you please organize for Tejas Sah to come to my office. Oh, and tell Mr Steele his pay rise and bonus have been cancelled.'

The principal then turned his gaze back to Xander.

'Now what to do with you … you're suspended from school for a week … and if you ever cheat at anything, I don't care if it's playing marbles, you will be expelled. Understood?'

'Understood.'

After leaving Mr Whisker's office, Xander let out a small sigh. *Suspended — Mum and Dad are going to kill me!* Then he thought about Phoebe, and smiled.

That night Xander was watching the local news with his parents when the familiar face of Senior Sergeant Dana Dawson appeared on the screen. She was being interviewed by a young reporter in front of the black lighthouse.

'… and if no one comes forward to claim the jewels, then

the Bungalow by the Beach can keep them,' said the police officer.

The camera then zoomed in to focus on the interviewer. 'This is wonderful timing, as according to those who run the charity, they were going to have to close their doors next month …' she said into the camera.

'That's fantastic news,' said Mr Beeston.

'Yeah, they do a great job for the kids,' said Mrs Beeston, giving her husband's hand a squeeze. Xander smiled.

'Hey, no smiling Mr Cheater!' said Mr Beeston.

The phone started ringing and Xander leapt from his chair.

'I'll get it — it's probably my parole officer,' he said. He raced over to pick up the phone and was surprised to hear Cat's voice.

'Hey Xander. Tee-Jay and I are trying to work out how to sneak into the cannery and find out what's under that trapdoor. Are you in?'

Xander's eyes sparkled as brightly as Finito's treasure.

'Definitely.'

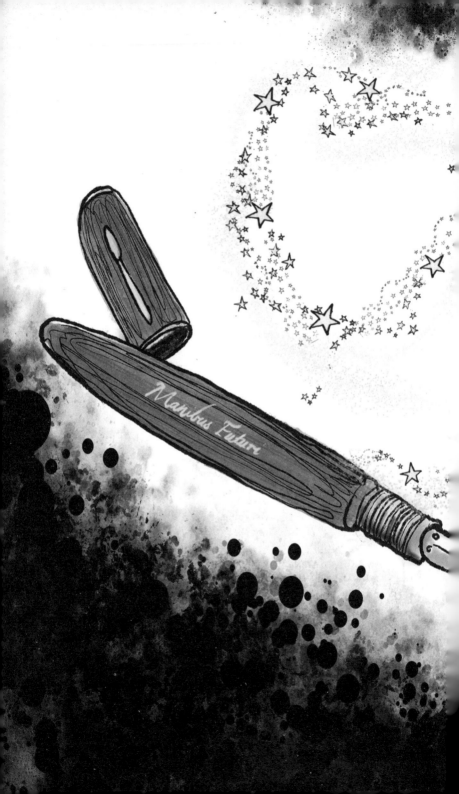

CHAPTER

16

The next night, Xander, Cat and Tee-Jay put their six-part plan into action.

Part one was particularly risky, as it involved riding up to the factory where two guards and a scary-looking Bullmastiff dog were located.

Xander peered around the gate before turning to give his friends a thumbs-up.

'Best of luck,' said Cat.

'You sure you don't want me to do this?' asked Tee-Jay.

Xander shook his head, then pedalled his bike through the gate.

'Oi! What are you doing? This is private property!' The angry security guard's words woke up the other guard, who had been sleeping in the chair next to him. 'I was only resting my eyes,' he said instinctively.

The Bullmastiff started a low growl and a thick stream of

drool began cascading from its mouth.

'I'm selling brownies to raise money for the Dukescliff Life Saving Club,' said Xander.

'We're not interested, so you can—'

'Wait a minute, Lenny,' said Bruno, the guard who'd just woken up. 'I'm feeling a little peckish, so let's have a look at them.'

Lenny rolled his eyes as Xander reached into his backpack.

He pulled out a pack of six dark-brown, moist-looking brownies, wrapped in clear plastic. Bruno's eyes widened and Xander thought he was about to start drooling like the guard dog.

'They look *okay*, I guess,' he said. 'How much?'

'Three dollars for the pack,' replied Xander.

'Three dollars! I'll pay *one* dollar.'

'You're haggling with a kid over charity brownies?' said Lenny, shaking his head.

'Take it or leave it,' said Bruno.

Xander reluctantly handed over the brownies and put the money into his pocket.

As he rode off he heard Bruno say, 'I knew he'd cave — sucker!'

When Xander rejoined Cat and Tee-Jay, it was time for part two of their plan: waiting.

The three friends lay on their stomachs and watched Bruno rip open the brownies and shove one into his mouth. He looked upwards and nodded enthusiastically before offering one to his co-worker.

Lenny hesitated briefly, then took it and had a nibble. He also nodded appreciatively, before finishing it off with one bite.

Xander smiled and silently high-fived Cat and Tee-Jay. He had always enjoyed making brownies using his mum's amazing recipe. But this special batch had an extra secret ingredient … laxatives!

In no time, all six brown treats were devoured. *Now the fun begins*, thought Xander.

Bruno started rubbing his stomach, then rushed inside. Less than a minute later, Lenny bolted after him.

'The toilets are at the far end of the factory,' whispered Tee-Jay. 'And to use them the guards will switch off the sensor alarm.'

'Reckon we've got about ten minutes,' said Cat as they rushed towards the door.

Time for part three of the plan! They slowed down as they approached the Bullmastiff, whose lead was tied loosely to a lamp post. The dog leaned forward and snarled.

'Easy boy. Easy,' said Cat in a calming voice. 'Look what

I've got for you.' She slowly pulled a juicy piece of steak from her backpack.

The muscular, fawn-coloured dog stopped snarling and started sniffing the air.

'That-a-boy,' said Cat tossing the meat to the dog's right. The Bullmastiff was so strong, his well-worn leather lead snapped as he bounded over to chomp into the steak.

Xander then led the way into the factory. The trapdoor was easy to find because Bruno had switched on the lights during his dash to the toilets. It was now time for part four of their plan.

Tee-Jay held up a pair of blue bolt cutters that he had 'borrowed' from his father's shed. He moved the sharp pincers toward the loop of metal on the trapdoor's padlock, then locked onto it.

Click! The loop snapped and Xander knelt down and removed the padlock. He looked up at his friends then pulled open the trapdoor.

Cat shone her torch into the square hole and Xander's eyes widened. Underneath the factory floor was a giant, rusty old steel tank.

Xander took out his 'soon to be sold' phone, to carry out part five of their plan: taking photos.

Once he was satisfied he'd captured some decent shots, he

whispered, 'Time for the final part of our plan — getting out of here!' He quietly lowered the trapdoor, got to his feet and … froze.

The Bullmastiff was standing a short distance away and he did not look happy. The dog let out a low-pitched growl then started barking wildly.

'What's going on out there?' yelled Bruno from the other end of the factory. The sound of a toilet flushing let Xander know they were only seconds away from being caught. And with a fierce dog blocking their only exit, there was no escape.

Suddenly, a second dog stormed through the factory door and started barking at the Bullmastiff.

'Shiver!' said Xander.

The two dogs bared their teeth and started circling each other.

The guard dog was so focused on Shiver that he completely ignored the three intruders as they sprinted for the exit. Xander made it to his bike with Cat and Tee-Jay hot on his heels, as the savage sound of fighting dogs trailed behind them. They peddled off into the night as fast as they could, and once they arrived at the footbridge, stopped to get their breath back.

'OMG!' said Cat. 'That dog saved us!'

'That was Shiver,' said Xander.

'Who?' asked Tee-Jay.

'He's my dog. Well, sort of. I just hope he's okay …'

Right on cue, a dog with reddish brown fur with white patches bounded towards him. It jumped up and licked his face.

'So good to see you boy!' Xander glanced down and noticed some blood on Shiver's rear right leg.

'You'd better come home with me tonight,' he said.

Shiver barked in agreement.

'So … what do we do now?' asked Tee-Jay.

'Tomorrow morning we're going to visit Mr Simmonds.'

'Who?' asked Cat.

'He used to own the Dukescliff general store before it was torn down to build the cannery,' explained Xander. 'And he lives at the end of my street.'

The next morning, Xander had a weird dream about being trapped inside a dishwasher. He woke to discover Shiver was licking his face.

'Stop it!'

This only seemed to encourage the dog, who let out a playful bark.

'Shhh!'

Suddenly Mr Beeston burst into the room.

'Is there a dog in here?'

Shiver gave Xander another lick on his face.

'Kind of.'

'Kind of? Pretty sure that's a dog on your bed, slobbering all over you ...'

'His name's Shiver and—'

'And he's got to go. Come on, let's get him outside now.'

'But he's injured ... and he saved my life!'

Shiver rolled over on the bed and looked up at Mr Beeston with his cute brown eyes.

'Oh, alright! We'll clean him up. But then he's gone.'

'Thanks, Dad.'

'Just don't tell your mother ...'

'Don't tell me *what*?' called out Mrs Beeston from the hallway.

'Um, how beautiful she is,' said Mr Beeston.

'Top save, Dad!'

'Top save *nothing*,' said Mrs Beeston poking her head inside the bedroom. 'I heard the whole thing.'

She walked over to inspect Shiver's wound.

'We'll need to sterilize that, then wrap a bandage around it. But first, let's clean him up in the bathroom.'

'Way ahead of you,' said Mr Beeston holding up some

towels he had grabbed from the hallway cupboard.

'Not the good towels, Cam!' said Mrs Beeston.

Xander laughed and gave Shiver a tickle under his chin.

'Hey Mum, is it okay if Cat, Tee-Jay and I go and visit Mr Simmonds this morning?'

'How come?'

'We want to ask him about his old general store.'

'History project?'

'Sort of.'

'Well okay — as long as you don't annoy him. There's some freshly baked tea cake in the kitchen you can take with you.'

'Thanks, Mum.'

Mrs Beeston turned to Shiver. 'Okay, let's get you cleaned up, mister.'

Xander shut the front door and began walking down Quarry Street holding a container filled with delicious tea cake. He spotted Cat and Tee-Jay sitting on their bikes in front of Mr Simmonds' neat orange brick home.

'Hey Xander,' said Tee-Jay.

'How's Shiver?' asked Cat.

'Mum and Dad are patching him up, but he's fine.'

Xander walked up the cement path bordered by colourful

red and yellow roses to the front door. He knocked three times and surveyed the tidy patio, noting a small hand-painted sign on the bricks that said 'Sea Haven'.

The bolt slid back and the door opened, revealing a skinny old man with grey wisps of hair. The man stared at Xander and the two children behind him.

'You're young Beeston, aren't you? Xander?'

'That's right, Mr Simmonds. Mum wanted me to give you some cake, and we … we wanted to ask you about your old general store.'

'Come on in,' said the man, shuffling towards his lounge room.

The inside of Mr Simmonds' home was as neat as the outside garden. It was clean and uncluttered, and Xander was surprised that the furniture was quite modern.

After directing his young visitors to sit on the couch, Mr Simmonds took the plastic container from Xander. 'Anyone want lemonade with their cake?' he asked. Three hands shot up in the air, causing Mr Simmonds to chuckle. He headed to the kitchen and soon returned carrying a tray with four full plastic cups and four slices of cake.

He placed the tray on a coffee table and said, 'Help yourselves.'

'Thanks,' said the three visitors, each grabbing the nearest cup.

'So you want to talk about my general store?'

'Yes,' said Xander, 'You used to serve petrol didn't you?'

Mr Simmonds nodded.

'And after you sold the business, what happened to the underground petrol tank?' asked Tee-Jay.

'Well, Tristan Clagg had to drain and remove it, as well as decontaminate the soil — it was part of the deal.'

'And did he?' asked Cat.

'He claimed he did ... I remember him complaining about how much it cost. He said the only upside was he wouldn't have to pay any tax for years.'

Xander pulled out his phone and walked over to Mr Simmonds.

'We took these photos at the factory last night ...'

He handed his phone to the old man, who started swiping through the images.

'That tank shouldn't be there. Or it should have at least been drained and sealed up properly ... and you can see from the leaks and the rust that it wasn't.'

'So could a fuel leak cause ground-water pollution?' asked Tee-Jay.

'That could kill animals?' added Cat.

'Definitely!'

'Cat, there was a funny smell at your farm when I saw that snake,' said Xander. 'It was like rotten eggs ... that could have been petrol.'

'That bit of bushland must be where the contaminated water is coming up,' said Tee-Jay.

'Which explains why the dam tested as normal — because it wasn't the water source that was killing the animals,' said Cat.

'Thanks heaps, Mr Simmonds,' said Xander. 'You've been a lot of help.'

'My pleasure,' chuckled the old man. 'Speaking of Tristan Clagg, do you want to see the video of your dad accidently conking him on the head with the sprinkler? I filmed the whole thing on my phone — was planning on sending it to one of those "funniest home videos" shows.'

'Yes I would,' said Xander with a smile. 'In fact, could you please send it to my phone?'

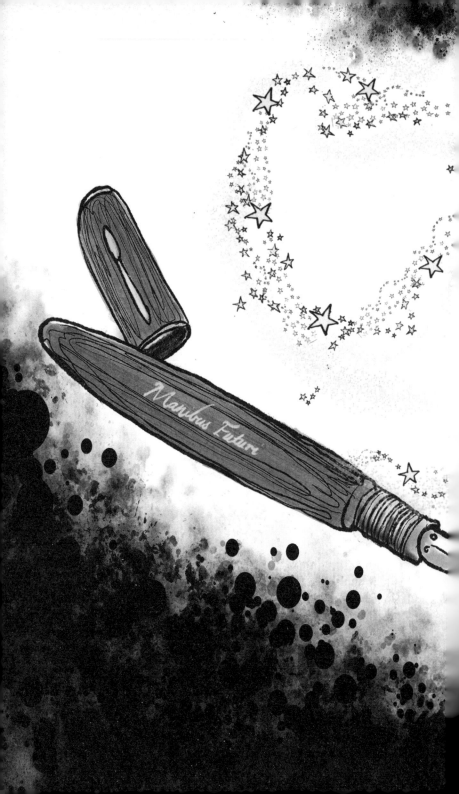

CHAPTER
17

When Xander arrived home from Mr Simmonds' place, his dad was talking in a strange voice. 'Who's a clever boy, hey? Who's a clever boy?'

His mum also sounded like she was speaking to a baby. 'You're soooo cute aren't you? Cutie, cutie, cutie.'

Xander followed their voices to the bathroom.

'You can tell he's super-smart,' said Mr Beeston.

'Definitely — it's in his eyes,' agreed Mrs Beeston.

Xander poked his head around the corner and saw his parents fawning over a spotlessly clean dog.

Shiver's tail was wagging and when he spotted Xander he let out a playful bark.

'It's like he can talk,' gushed Mr Beeston.

'Xander, we've decided it's best if Shiver stays with us for now … you know, until his leg heals.'

'Yes, we couldn't send an injured animal back into the

wild,' said Mr Beeston. He then looked at Shiver and put on his 'weird' voice again. 'Could we? No we couldn't!'

Xander decided to leave his parents before they started blowing raspberries on Shiver's tummy. He went to his bedroom, pulled out his phone and began sending the photos from the cannery, along with Mr Simmonds' video, to his laptop.

He then typed up an email exactly as he had discussed with Cat and Tee-Jay.

Hey Senior Sergeant Dawson,

Firstly, we want to report a crime. There is a leaky, toxic petrol tank under a trapdoor in Clagg's Cannery. Mr Clagg told everyone he removed this twenty years ago, but as the photos below prove, he never did.

As a result, we believe he has contaminated some underground water that bubbled up on the Cruzes' farm, killing several much-loved alpacas, as well as innocent birds and reptiles (including a red bellied snake).

And secondly we have attached a video (taken by Mr Simmonds) that shows exactly what happened the day Mr Clagg said he was assaulted. This proves Mr Beeston is innocent.

Thanks,
Catalina (Cat) Cruz
Tejas (Tee-Jay) Sah
Xander Beeston

Xander moved the curser so that it hovered over the send button. 'Fingers crossed,' he whispered.

Click. Swoosh.

As the email sped off to the Dukescliff police station, Mr Beeston called out from the bathroom. 'We're taking Shiver for a walk if you want to come along. Then we have to tidy up the house — your sister comes home from hospital tomorrow.'

Xander smiled. 'Count me in!'

Xander put down Phoebe's bag and opened the front door. 'After you, sis.'

'It's good to be home,' she said.

Phoebe rolled inside and was instantly confronted by a dog bounding up the hallway. Shiver jumped up onto the wheelchair and started licking her face.

Phoebe shrieked then started laughing uncontrollably. 'Who's this?' she squealed.

'Get down, Shiver! You're Mummy's naughty little boy, aren't you! Aren't you!' said Mrs Beeston.

'Yes you are. Yes you are!' cooed Mr Beeston.

Xander looked at Phoebe and raised his eyebrows. 'Um, this is Shiver. Mum and Dad said we could keep him while he recovers.'

'Your father's going to put an ad in the paper to see if he belongs to someone … eventually,' explained Mrs Beeston.

'He's very smart, Phoebs,' said Mr Beeston. I've already taught him a few tricks. Watch this! Roll over! Come, Shiver, roll over …'

Shiver cocked his head to one side and stared at Mr Beeston.

'See! He started to roll his head,' declared Mr Beeston.

'Clever boy, Shiver,' said Mrs Beeston.

Both parents then puckered their lips and started making kissing sounds.

'Phoebs, how about we take your bags to your room?' suggested Xander.

'Please!' she replied.

As they headed past the lounge room, Phoebe smiled.

'Our old TV and couch are back … and it looks like The Seeker's been dusted off,' she said.

'Yeah, Dad still reckons he's going to find Finito's treasure — even though it's already been discovered!'

'As if Finito would have only buried *one* lot of treasure!' called out Mr Beeston.

Xander put Phoebe's bag on her bed and said, 'Can I show you something?'

'Sure.'

He led his sister to his room and turned on his computer.

'Here's an email we sent to the police yesterday. Cat told me they were on the farm investigating this morning.'

'That is so cool, Xander.'

'And Senior Sergeant Dawson rang Dad to say that after Mr Clagg saw Mr Simmonds' embarrassing video, he dropped the charges immediately.'

'I'm proud of you, bro.'

'Thanks. But the main thing I want to show you is *this* …'

Xander pressed 'return' on his keyboard and Phoebe's eyes widened.

'Is that a …'

'… crowd-funding page. I've been working on it for a while and wanted to check with you before uploading it.'

Phoebe started reading out the words that were under the

heading: 'Kinista for my Sister'.

> My sister Phoebe is amazing. She had a bike acci-
> dent and ended up in a wheelchair but has never
> complained once. She has taught me so much
> (even though I'm her older brother!) and now I'd
> like to do something for her. There's this clinical
> trial called Kinista 99 which could help her to walk
> again. Pretty cool, right? The only problem is it
> costs two hundred thousand dollars for six months
> treatment, which is two hundred thousand dol-
> lars more than my family has right now. If you can
> donate any amount of money, that would really
> make a difference. If you ever meet Phoebe, you'll
> see how incredible she is — I'm very lucky to have
> her as my sister.
> Xander Beeston, twelve years old.

Phoebe looked up at her brother with tears in her eyes.

'Thanks Xander … of course you can upload it. That's amazing.'

'It'll be hard to raise that much money but …'

'That doesn't matter, bro. I'm planning on an exciting future whether I'm in a chair or not. The fact that you've done this for me is special enough — so thanks.'

The emotional moment was interrupted by Mrs Beeston shouting in the hallway.

'No, Shiver! Not in the hallway. Bad dog!'

'Don't worry honey, I've got this — it's only a small puddle,' said Mr Beeston.

'Not the good towels, Cam!'

Xander looked at his sister and they both burst out laughing.

At dinner the next night, Xander tapped his glass.

'Ahem! I have some big news. And by big, I mean "good".'

'So have I,' said Phoebe.

Then Mr Beeston looked at Mrs Beeston and said, 'So have we!'

'But we've also got some bad news,' said Mrs Beeston.

'Oh yeah,' said Mr Beeston. 'Okay, you start Phoebs, then Xander, then we'll finish off.'

'Okay, so Riverview Grammar emailed me and … even though I can't run any more, they're going to continue my scholarship through to my final year.'

'Woohoo!' said Xander as Mr and Mrs Beeston burst into applause.

'I'm *so* glad you'll be moving back to the city,' said Xander.

'That's not very nice,' said Phoebe with a grin.

'Because that's where you'll be starting your Kinista 99 clinical trial!'

'No way!'

'Yes way! The family whose baby you saved donated twenty-five thousand dollars, and we reached two hundred thousand dollars within three hours!'

'Thanks big bro … just … thanks,' said Phoebe with tears in her eyes.

Xander had already told his parents about the crowdfunding campaign, but they did a great job at pretending to be surprised.

'We're so proud of you, Xander,' said Mrs Beeston.

'He gets it from his father, you know,' said Mr Beeston. Mrs Beeston immediately pretended to choke on her Brussels sprouts, causing everyone to burst out laughing.

'Okay Dad, what's *your* big news?' asked Xander.

'Senior Sergeant Dawson came to the factory today and you'll never guess what she did!'

'Opened a trapdoor and discovered a leaky petrol tank that Mr Clagg was supposed to have removed twenty years ago?'

'Well yes … but that's serious because—'

'The petrol seeped into the waterways and killed alpacas on the Cruzes' farm?' said Phoebe.

'Um, yes … but there was also a twist—'

'Because Mr Clagg lied about paying money to clean up the site, so he's in trouble for tax fraud,' said Xander.

'Sure … but the upshot of all this was—'

'Mr Clagg got arrested!' said Xander and Phoebe together.

'You guys are no fun at all!' complained Mr Beeston.

'But what was the bad news?' asked Xander.

'Well, as Tristan was being taken away in handcuffs, he started screaming about shutting the factory down so that everyone would lose their jobs,' explained Mrs Beeston. There was a lull in the conversation as the impact of this news sunk in.

'So … why don't the workers buy the factory and run it themselves?' asked Xander.

Phoebe nodded enthusiastically, and Mr and Mrs Beeston looked at each other and chuckled.

'It doesn't work like that, kids,' said Mr Beeston.

'That's right,' agreed Mrs Beeston. 'It's not that simple.'

'Why not?' asked Xander.

'Well, for starters we'd all have to borrow lots of money,' said Mr Beeston.

'Isn't that what banks are for?' said Phoebe.

'True … but why would Tristan sell to us?' said Mrs Beeston.

'He mightn't have a choice,' said Xander. 'He's going to need money to pay the fines and clean up the mess he's made.'

'I suppose … but who'd run the place?'

'Don't the workers already do all the work?'

'That's true, Cam,' said Mrs Beeston. 'What did Tristan and Portia really do?'

Mr Beeston furrowed his brow. 'Well, Tristan played golf every day, and Portia went to lunch with her friends all afternoon … yeah, what did they do?'

'I'll make a few calls,' said Mrs Beeston, 'And Cam, you have a chat to Mrs McNamara next door — she's an accountant …'

A week later, Xander and Phoebe arranged to meet their parents at Clagg's Cannery after work so they could take Shiver for a family walk.

The sun was beginning to set on Cygnet Bay as Xander fought to control Shiver on a leash. Phoebe looked over at the enthusiastic dog as she rolled along beside him.

'Aww, he's keen to see his mummy and daddy,' she said, impersonating her father. 'Yes he is. Yes he is!'

Xander laughed and high-fived his sister.

'Do you think the workers voted to buy the factory?' he asked.

Phoebe pointed to the sign in the distance. 'Yep!'

Xander squinted and saw that 'Clagg's' had been crossed out and replaced by 'Dukescliff'. And underneath 'Cannery', the word 'Co-op' had been added.

'Cool,' said Xander.

They walked through the gates and as they approached the factory, Xander turned to Phoebe. 'There's something I need to do before we see Mum and Dad,' he said.

With Shiver loping alongside him, Xander led his sister through the door and over to the crushing machine. It was making a lot of noise as it was currently pulverizing an assortment of waste.

Xander took the pen from his pocket and Shiver immediately started barking.

'It's okay, boy,' he said.

He studied the pen one last time, and said, 'Thank you.'

With a flick of his wrist, he tossed the pen into the crushing machine and listened to the sound of the pen being destroyed.

'Why did you say thank you?' asked Phoebe.

'Because I'm not afraid anymore.'

Phoebe nodded and smiled. 'Not all superheroes have big muscles,' she said.

'What do you mean?' joked Xander. He started doing ridiculous body-building poses just as his parents arrived.

'Put those guns away!' said Mr Beeston. 'Your mother has some exciting news — she's been elected general manager of the co-op!'

'Wow!' said Xander. 'Does that mean she can sack you, Dad?'

'She'd never do that … would you, honey?'

Mrs Beeston shrugged her shoulders. 'Maybe …'

Mr Beeston turned to Xander and his sister, and gave them a wink. 'Knew I shouldn't have voted for her!'

They all burst out laughing, apart from Shiver, who barked and wagged his tail.

Epilogue

In Cranford the next day …

The thick mist that had suddenly descended over the marketplace gave Finn his chance.

He could not see his foster parents, which hopefully meant they could not see him. As he dropped to the ground and started crawling, he heard Mr Grimshaw's raspy voice. 'Finnian! Don't you dare go anywhere!'

'If you don't answer right now, you'll pay for it later,' hissed Mrs Grimshaw.

Finn kept crawling. People chatted, squealed and laughed around him, but he was totally focused on escaping. He had to get away from the Grimshaws and track down his real parents. He had to find out what had happened to him …

'Ow!' he said after colliding with the legs of a trestle table. As he climbed to his feet he bumped his head on the underside of the table. 'Double ow!'

He looked around and raised his eyebrows. The visibility in his immediate area was surprisingly good, given the rest of the marketplace was still completely blanketed in a pea soup fog.

Epilogue

His first instinct was to run away for fear of being spotted, but a gold flash of light from the table he'd bumped his head on grabbed his attention. It appeared to come from a pen. A strange old pen with gold writing on the side. He felt his hand being drawn towards it and …

Zap! A warm burst of energy leapt from the pen and quickly spread throughout his body. For the first time in his life Finn felt safe, as if he was wearing an invisible suit of armour.

'Nothing can harm me,' he whispered.

Also in this series …

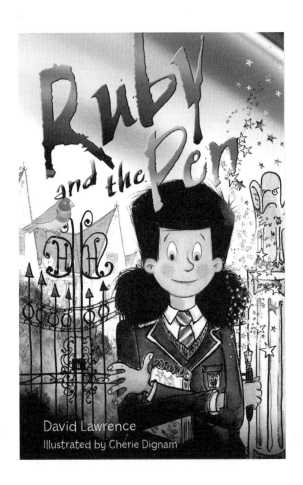